PHOENIX FATALE

NATHAN GOODMAN

THOUGHT REACH PRESS

THOUGHT REACH PRESS

United States of America

First Thought Reach Press printing, August 2018.

ALSO BY NATHAN GOODMAN

Also by USA Today Bestselling Author Nathan Goodman

The Special Agent Jana Baker Spy-Thriller Series

Protocol One

The Fourteenth Protocol

Protocol 15

Breach of Protocol

Rendition Protocol

Get a Free Copy of

Protocol One

Details at the end of this book

1

CRITICAL CONDITION

Pearland, Texas, south of Houston
  Late September

"Dammit! Where's my blood type? She's going to bleed out," said Dr. Ken Brantley -- the attending E.R. physician at the Pearland Medical Center -- to a team of frantic medical personnel. "Tell the lab to expedite. Let's do a CVC, chem panel, and tox screen to see if she's on anything. Where the hell did she come from anyway? If she didn't get here by ambulance, how did we get her?"

There was no answer.

"Doctor, her face," a young nurse said. "My God, look at her face." She wrung her hands as she backed away.

"Animals," came his reply. "The damage to her facial structure is the least of her problems right now. We've got to get her stable. Kelly, get back over here. She's not going to hurt you."

But the young nurse froze, her eyes wide.

Dr. Brantley quieted his tone and tried again. "Kelly, she's a person. She's a human being with a mother and a father and people who love her. She needs your help."

The nurse complied.

"Doctor," yelled a lab technician from across the room, "she's type O-positive. The chem panel and tox screen will be out momentarily."

"All right, let's start her on two liters of O-positive with lactated ringers. I don't like the look of this," he said. "Her blood pressure is dropping, people. She's losing blood somewhere." He glanced at the heart monitor. It painted a jagged line across the screen. "She's tacky. Shit, she's going into V-fib! Get the crash cart. Charge, three hundred."

The fledgling nurse stared at him, again frozen.

"Kelly!" His thunderous voice awakened her from a state of mental vapor-lock. Kelly spun around, grabbed the defibrillator cart, and wheeled it into position. "Charging three hundred," she said across shaky vocal cords.

The doctor took the paddles, applied them to the young female patient's chest and yelled, "Clear!"

The body rocked upward as everyone studied the heart monitor. "Thank God. Normal sinus rhythm. That was close."

"Chem panel toxicology results are back," a technician said

"Well, what is it?"

"No barbiturates or other illegal narcotics, but she drew a positive test for Rohypnol."

"Roofies. Son of a bitch, the date rape drug. Somebody ought to find the thug that did this to her and kick his ass."

"Looks like someone's way ahead of you, doc," said the same lab tech. "Just saw a bunch of cops come in with the medics. They're bringing in four more, males, unconscious. Pretty banged up from the looks of them. Ambulance driver said he doesn't know anything about our female patient here, but he picked up the others at a biker bar."

"Well maybe there is a little justice in the world," Dr. Brantley said. He took an ultrasound wand in his hand, pressed it into the woman's abdomen and rotated it from one side to the next. "Call Surgery. Tell them we're sending one up."

"What is it?" Kelly said.

"Here, learn something. See this?" he said as he pointed at the ultrasound monitor. "That's her spleen. See the cloudy area here, on the edge? That's a rupture. Tell the O.R. we've got to expedite on this one. This young lady is going to be lucky if she survives the night."

As the staff wheeled the patient from the room, the physician turned and said, "Now, let's go take a look at the thugs."

2

THE MYSTERIOUS DROP OFF

"I don't know where she came from," the hospital insurance administrator said.

"So, at this point, we don't even have an ID on her?" her supervisor replied.

"No, nothing. She apparently had no ID on her person when she arrived. And, no one seems to know how she got into the hospital in the first place. It says on the report that the patient is in critical condition. I hardly believe she walked in here under her own power."

"Great, another Jane Doe," the supervisor said. "Like this hospital can withstand another patient we can't collect a dime from. This is ridiculous. Call hospital security. Ask them to find out how she got here. Somebody has to know. Maybe we can reach her next of kin."

* * *

An hour later, two hospital security officers walked into the administrator's office. "Strangest patient arrival I've ever seen," one said.

"It's like this, Dr. Cook," the other said. "As you know, we've got security officers patrolling the hospital at regular intervals. But we also have one or two others monitoring security cameras at all times. That being said, with so many cameras and so few officers, it's hard to catch everything."

"So, what happened?" the administrator said.

"Well, at 11:32 p.m. we get an alarm on port 266. That's a service door over on the west side of the hospital. You know, it's a door leading to the outside, down the alley? Anyway, the alarm on that door sounded, so we dispatched an officer to check it out."

"And?"

"The officer radios back that he's got a dead body lying in the hallway just inside the door."

"A dead body?"

"It turns out he just *thought* the person was dead. Think about it; he responded to the door alarm and finds this woman lying there, all bloodied up. But, it was your Jane Doe. She was barely alive. Scared the shit out of him though."

"Yeah, I bet. So, what are you telling me? That she walked in the door and collapsed? In her condition?"

"No, ma'am. There's no way."

The physician administrator, Dr. Elaine Cook, pursed her lips and shifted in her seat. "And why not?"

"Like you said. She was in no condition to open any

door. Hell, she wasn't even conscious. And, that door is sealed. There's no way to open it from the outside."

"Why, because she didn't have a key?"

"There's no keyhole on the outside of that door anyway. It doesn't even have a door handle on that side. There's no way to open it. It has to be opened from the inside. But somehow, someone did. Someone else got in that door, and they did it from the alley."

"How do you know someone on the inside didn't open it?"

"Inside the building, motion sensors on the hallway security camera covering that door would have tripped. The camera is way up the hallway from the door. If anyone inside the hospital walked down that hall toward the door, the camera would have recorded it. But there's nothing." The security supervisor held up his hands. "I know, I know. It's not making any sense to me either. Here's what I do know. Somehow, someone opened that door from the outside -- a door that has no keylock and no door handle -- and dumped her inside without being detected. Hold on a second, we're pulling up security video from the camera pointed at that alleyway outside the door. You got it yet, Charlie?" he said to a uniformed man with a mustard stain on his name badge.

"Yeah, but it doesn't show much," Charlie said. "See here? It's dark as hell out there, but there's definitely somebody in that alleyway, carrying something heavy over his shoulder. But you can't see nothin'. It's just his silhouette."

The administrator was incredulous. "So, some guy pops

open an un-openable door and drops a critically wounded patient inside our building, what, so the alarm would sound, and we'd find her?"

"Sure would have been easier to use the Emergency Room entrance," the first security officer said.

"Unless you didn't want anyone to know who you were," Charlie replied.

MEDICAL CONDITION

"All right, let's do some triage here, people," Dr. Brantley said. "The most critical go first. We have four victims?"

"I don't think you'd want to call these members of a biker gang 'victims' doc," a man standing against the wall in a rumpled business suit said. A badge hung from his jacket pocket. "These are the attackers."

"Whatever," Dr. Brantley replied. "Okay, so what have we got?" he said to a team of nurses and residents. "Come on, call them out."

"Multiple contusions on this one," a medical resident said. "His face looks crushed on this side. From the way he's wheezing, I'd say he's got a collapsed lung."

"This one's unconscious," another young doctor said. "His left leg has a compound fracture at the knee, which is totally inverted, by the way."

"Same here. This one is unconscious as well, but both the

left knee and right elbow are compound fractured and totally inverted."

"What about that last one?" Brantley asked.

"Not a priority," another resident said. "He's DOA."

"Start with number one," Dr. Brantley ordered. "Let's get in a chest tube. You know the drill. Move, people." The doctor sat back and watched his team. This was the perfect training scenario.

The detective stepped forward. "Doc, I don't think I have to tell you, but I'm investigating an attack on a female that occurred at a biker bar on the east end of town. These look like our perps. I know you've got to get them stabilized, but I want them tested. I mean it, as soon as they're stable, I want their genital regions swabbed for DNA. Their bodies are a crime scene. Got it?"

"No problem. The female victim came in just before they did. As soon as she's out of surgery, they'll run a rape kit on her."

"Witnesses at the bar say there's no doubt she was attacked. How is the victim, by the way? I need to talk to her."

"You can talk to her if she survives."

"It's that bad?"

The doctor's answer came in the form of a stern gaze.

"Hey, doc," the detective said. "The witnesses also said another individual, a male subject, got in a fight with these four and saved the girl. Apparently, he's the one who caused all this damage. There's no way he fought off all of these guys without sustaining injuries himself. You got anybody else in here within the last forty-five minutes that might be our guy?"

"No, but you can talk to hospital security. The hospital admin was down here a while ago and told me an unidentified male broke into a side entrance off the alley and dropped your female victim off."

"You're kidding. Thanks, doc. And doc? Here's my card. Call me if you get anyone in here that might be our guy."

Dr. Brantley nodded as he glanced at the card. The card read 'Lt. Dan T. Whelan, Detective. Special Victims Unit.'

LOYALTY TO WOMEN

Detective Dan Whelan stood in the hospital security office and watched the video surveillance tape. And just as the doctor had told him, he observed a male subject walk down the alley, enter the locked door, then drop the female victim inside.

She was officially known as 'Jane Doe' on the hospital charts, and Whelan intended on finding out who she was, and what had happened inside that bar.

He got in his car and headed back to Chopper Town, Pearland, Texas' most notorious biker bar. When he arrived, police cruisers were everywhere. Throngs of the bar's patrons were divided into small groups, each being interviewed by a uniformed officer or detective.

Whelan lifted a section of crime scene tape and walked underneath. Inside, more crime scene tape separated the back room of the club from the smoke-filled pool table area in the front.

"What do we have, Bill?" Whelan said.

"The tape from the security camera in here sucks, but you won't believe what you *do* see on it."

"Give me the annotated version. She was gang-raped?"

"No doubt. Beaten pretty badly. The strange thing is, she doesn't look like a girl you'd normally see in a place like this."

"How so?"

"The way she was dressed. High-class, for sure. No one here had ever seen her before tonight. And other things, like the hairstyle. Not to mention that she's got all her teeth. Well, she had all of them, anyway. Sorry, don't mean to be so crude. At any rate, they all say 'city' to me. Definitely not a biker babe."

"So, what is it you want me to see on the tape?"

"It's the fight that ensued after a lone subject walked into view to stop them," Bill said.

"What about it?"

"Let me put it this way. You had four biker gang members at the emergency room, right?"

"Yeah, and one of them was DOA."

"Well, there's three more DOA's here."

"What? No one told me there were three more bodies here."

"Yeah, and I shouldn't call them 'dead on arrivals;' I'd say they were more like 'killed in action.'"

"I don't follow," Whelan said

"The difference is that our hero, if that's what you want to call him, would make Rambo look like a pussy. He's ex-military for sure. From the way he mowed through these guys, I'd say he's special ops, maybe Navy SEALs, or Army Delta Force. I've never seen anything like it."

"Holy shit."

"Yeah," Bill replied. "And the three dead guys in here? They all look like someone smashed their heads in with a sledgehammer. But the security camera shows he used no weapons, other than his hands and feet, that is. All their necks are broken too."

They walked to the manager's office and the two detectives watched and re-watched the surveillance video. The man, who had moved in to stop the attack on Jane Doe, looked like something out of the movie *The Terminator*; a mass of lean muscle covering bones of steel. It didn't appear as though he had an ounce of body-fat on him.

"My God," Whelan said. "It's not that he just went in to stop these guys from raping her. He went in there with the express purpose to kill them all, like he snapped or something. If he doesn't turn up at the hospital tonight, we'll need to build a psychological profile on him. He must have a fierce sense of loyalty to women or something. I'd bet he comes from a bad home, you know, somewhere where the father beat the mother? All that shit."

"Kind of rare these days."

"No kidding," Whelan replied.

"You're right," Bill said. "Once he saw what they were doing to her, he wasn't going to let any of them escape. I mean, look at how he grabbed this guy here who was trying to get away."

"The victim, Jane Doe, we need an identity on her. She might not make it. The hospital is desperate to find any family members. No one here's ever seen her before? Maybe you're right," he said as he looked at Bill. "Maybe she didn't frequent shit-holes like this."

"But what would make a girl like that come in here in the first place? I mean, it's not safe, obviously. And look around. It's a dump. Why risk it?"

Whelan answered, "I don't know. But then again, we've seen this kind of behavior before, right? You know, sometimes a perfectly normal woman gets a thing in her head and decides she wants a biker dude. I don't know, it's the danger or something that turns them on."

* * *

A few hours later, as Whelan and the other officers gathered evidence at the crime scene, Whelan's cell phone rang.

"Whelan," he said into the phone.

"Detective? This is Dr. Ken Brantley, Pearland Medical Center. We spoke earlier this evening?"

"Yes, Dr. Brantley. Did my suspect make it into your emergency room?"

"No. We didn't see anyone that even remotely looked like they'd just annihilated four gang members."

"Seven."

"Seven?" the doctor said.

"Yeah, there are three other DRT's down here at the biker bar, Rigg's said, using the cop slang for Dead Right There. "Anyway, what about Jane Doe? How's she doing?"

"Still alive, anyway. She's out of surgery. Lost her spleen, severe concussion. Several bones are crushed in her facial area. And yes, she drew a positive on the rape kit. All of the bikers have been genitally swabbed to collect evidence, and from the looks of it, I'd say these are definitely your guys. The state forensic lab will have to confirm it, obviously."

"Is she going to survive?" Whelan said.

"It's too soon to tell," the doctor answered.

"Is she conscious?"

"No, and if she does pull through, she won't be conscious for quite a while. She's been placed in a medically-induced coma. The surgeons were concerned about the swelling in her brain. They'll keep her sedated for a while to see if it dissipates. She seems like a fighter though. If I were a betting man, I'd say she'll make it."

"Doc?" Whelan said. "What about the bikers that came into the ER? What's their condition? They looked pretty bad."

"No kidding. I spoke to the orthopedic surgeon. He said he'd only ever seen joint breakages that bad in car accidents. Never as the result of a fight. It would take an awful lot of skill and rage to smash a knee or elbow joint so hard that it snapped backward."

"Yeah, I watched it on surveillance tape. Thanks for calling, Doc. Let me know how our girl is doing, okay? And Doc?"

"Yeah?"

"I'm going to nail these sons of bitches that attacked her."

5

UNJUST

Whiskey Rock Bar, Hollister, California.

The pool stick drove the cue ball into the rack so hard that pool balls shot in all directions and bounced off the bumpers, several dropping into holes. Gang member Paul Pliskin had been called 'Gears' for so long that none of the members of the Lincoln Killers actually remembered his first name anymore. Gears held a prestigious position in the gang, an elected position known as "Enforcer."

In a biker gang, enforcers are thought of as policemen, although that term is never used. It's the job of the enforcer to ensure order at regular club meetings, which are euphemistically referred to as "holding church." The enforcer is also in charge of security at gang events. But in the case of the Lincoln Killers, Gears Pliskin had another role, one not so commonly known. It was his job to do the bidding of the president, Michael John Brewer.

Brewer had been the president for three years running, and his power base continued to grow month after month. Like most members of the gang, Brewer was never referred to using his real name. He was known simply as "Grinder," a nickname he had earned in the early days. Back then, it was rumored that, in order to collect on a debt, he had shoved a man's hand into an industrial coffee grinder. After that, collecting past-due notes became easy. Grinder's reputation as a ruthless outlaw grew, and so did his popularity with fellow gang members. He challenged the then-president to a bare-knuckle fight -- and won. The Lincoln Killers had a new, de facto, president, and under his rule, the nationally organized gang flourished.

"Damn, Gears," Grinder said, "leave a man a few balls on the table next time."

A few other gang members, known as "patches," stepped back or to the side. They wanted to observe Grinder in action but understood to keep their distance.

Gears looked up but knew better than to challenge the boss. He leaned across the table and took his next shot. When it missed, Grinder sneered.

Grinder turned the Budweiser Tall Boy up and drained its contents. When the bottle was empty, he flung it across the bar, and it smashed into the cinder block wall at the back. The place was crowded at that time, but the occurrence of a flying beer bottle was so common few people looked up.

Grinder lined up his pool cue and began to drop one pool

ball after another into the pockets. As he lined up his last shot, he said, "So you're telling me we've got trouble?"

"That's right, boss," Gears replied.

Grinder dropped the eight-ball into a pocket, then stood tall. "And some sonofabitch killed three of our boys?"

"Not three," Gears said. "Seven."

Several patches, regular members of the club, and one other, known as a hang around, a prospective gang member still working off his initiation period, looked up.

"Seven?" Grinder said. "What the fuck do you mean, *seven*?"

"It's like this, boss. They were having a little fun with some whore at a bar at a place called Pearland, Texas. Then some big dude started a brawl with them. Four of our guys died right there. Four others made it to the hospital, but three went tits up as well."

Grinder raised the pool cue over his head and smashed it into the table. It snapped in half and splinters of wood flew in all directions. "Goddamnit! You mean to tell me one man killed seven of our brothers?"

Gears held still. It was his direct experience that when the boss got like this, a person could end up knocked unconscious, or worse. He nodded. "It looks that way."

Grinder walked away from the others. Gears set down his pool cue and followed. When the two of them were in a dark corner of the biker bar, Grinder grabbed the edge of a small wooden table and tipped it upright until the glasses and bottles on it dumped onto the ground. He and Gears sat. "So, let me see if I've got this straight. Eight of our boys get onto this slut, and some guy takes them on, and now seven of them are dead? One guy, one whore, and what, one surviving patch?"

"That about sums it up, boss," Gears said.

Grinder slammed his fist onto the table. "And who is this dead man that dared challenge the Lincoln Killers?"

"No one knows. The whole thing was caught on surveillance tape though. Cops are looking for him too."

"And the bitch?"

"Still alive. Though not by much."

Grinder leaned forward and spoke through gritted teeth. "Those dumbasses left a fucking whore to testify? What the hell is wrong with our chapter in Pearland, Texas?" He stood and began to storm off but stopped. "Send out a few scouts to Pearland. I have a feeling we're going to have to make a road trip."

6

ONE WEEK LATER

Pearland Medical Center.

"So, she's lucid now?" a male nurse said in the intensive care unit, staring at Jane Doe.

"Yes, they pulled her off the propofol this morning," another nurse replied. "She started regaining consciousness around two a.m."

"And is she talking?"

"Yes, but only in fits and starts. They've got her on a morphine drip which keeps her pretty groggy. She keeps saying 'he saved me, he saved me.' That's all we've gotten out of her so far."

"Who? You mean the guy on the news they keep calling 'The Terminator'?"

"I don't know. I guess so." Both nurses heard mumbling

sounds coming from the patient. "Shhh, she's saying some-thing." They leaned closer to her.

"He visits me, you know," Jane Doe said, though her eyes were still closed. "He visits me." A smile peeled across her bruised and swollen face. "Here in the hospital. He comes to visit me."

The two nurses looked at each other.

"Who does, honey? Who visits you?" one of the nurses said.

"He saved me. Those men, they were hurting me. But he saved me. He came in and tore them off of me."

"The man that saved you comes and visits you here in the hospital?" The nurses exchanged glances again.

"Late at night. You'll see. He doesn't want me to tell anybody though." She giggled as a devious, drunken little grin painted across her face.

As Jane Doe dozed back to sleep, the female nurse said, "She's out of it, all right. Ain't nobody visiting her late at night. Must be the morphine talking."

An hour and a half later several other nurses were in the middle of a shift change. A physician entered the floor while reading a chart. He was draped in blue-green surgical scrubs including cap and booties. He breezed past the patient rooms and stopped at a nurse's station with his head buried in the clipboard. Without uttering a word, he walked up to one of the hospital desktop computers and tapped the keyboard several times. The chart on Jane Doe popped onto the screen.

"Can I help you, doctor?" said an attractive blonde nurse just starting her shift.

"Just checking in on our girl," the physician replied as he pointed through the glass toward Jane Doe.

He studied the computer monitor a moment, then rose and walked into Jane Doe's room. At her bedside, he placed his hand in hers, then squeezed. His touch was warm, firm, and reassuring.

"I knew you'd come," Jane Doe whispered, though her eyes remained closed.

"How are you feeling?"

"Stronger. Much stronger."

"Good. I'm glad. But this is the last time I'm going to visit you."

"But . . ."

"No buts. The risk-reward ratio isn't high enough," he said. "When you're discharged, when you're at home, I'll come. I'll come to you, and we'll start. It's going to take a lot of work, but if you listen to me and learn what I teach you, nothing bad will ever happen to you again."

He turned and walked out. After he was down the hallway and had pushed through the heavy door into the stairwell, the blonde nurse said to the other, "Who is that physician? I've never seen him before."

"Which one?"

"The one that visits Jane Doe sometimes."

"Girl," the other said with a little smirk, "you just want

to meet him, don't you? I can see you; yes, I can. I can see you, and you want to get to know him just a little bit better." Her laughter was infectious.

"Oh, stop." It was a playful response. "Did you see his eyes? I could get lost in those eyes. And his hands. They look so . . . firm. It's like he's all covered up, but you can just tell, can't you?"

"Tell what?"

"Oh, come on. Like you don't notice his body. I bet he's a sculpted piece of man under there."

They both laughed.

THE SEARCH

Pearland Police Department

"All right, we've finally identified our victim, the one we been calling Jane Doe," Detective Whelan said as he breezed into the captain's office. "She regained consciousness after they took her off the meds. Her real name is Peyton Phoenix."

The captain looked up from the sea of paperwork piled on his desk. His short-sleeved button-down was wrinkled, and his comb-over had fallen to the side. He began speed talking. "Victim? What victim? We have another victim? Dammit, why wasn't I notified? The next time I'm not notified I'm going to kick somebody's ass."

"Whoa, whoa, whoa. Slow down there, Captain McJump-ToConclusions. Let's just take a breather." Whelan started laughing. "I'm talking about the rape victim from Chopper Town, that biker bar out on Dixie Farm Road by the airport. The gang-rape case. Jesus, boss, you'd think you'd remember that one. It's been on the news every day since it happened."

"Oh, yeah. The one with the Terminator guy who annihilated all the bikers. Got it. What's the situation on the case? Have you charged the bikers in the assault? How many were still alive after the Terminator got ahold of them? Have any leads? Do we know his ID? Dammit, man, I want answers."

"Geez, boss. You need a vacation. Slow down, already. All right, the answer to your first question is yes. I've charged the surviving biker with felony rape and attempted murder. He's got multiple felony priors, and since the surveillance video captured the entire event, I'd say it's a slam dunk. He won't see the light of day from outside of prison ever again. There was just the one survivor, by the way. One survivor out of *eight*. And no, we don't have an ID on our Terminator. I don't know, boss; it's like tracking down a ghost."

"Oh, don't give me that crap. How hard could it be? A public bar, fingerprints, video surveillance, witnesses. What's the big deal? Bring him in already. The district attorney wants to prosecute him."

"Prosecute him for what? Saving a twenty-three-year-old woman from being murdered after they finished gang-raping her?"

"Don't hand me that vigilante hero crap. It's right there on the video surveillance tape. He didn't just stop these guys from attacking her. He took them apart, piece by piece. And once he'd knocked them half unconscious, he snapped their necks like they were pretzels. It was systematic. That's murder in my book."

"Heat of the moment, I say. Captain, I'm being serious here. Does anyone besides you and the D.A. know that they want to prosecute him?"

"No, why?"

"Because if the public finds out, we're going to have to put on the riot gear. People will tear down the walls of this place. You ever seen an angry mob of women? It's scary. It'll be pandemonium."

"The law is the law. And there won't be any riots or protests or any of that."

"Oh, no?" Whelan continued. "The Terminator guy is so popular in the press right now, he's got a fan club page on Facebook. Over seventeen thousand likes so far. The page is raising money for women's rights. It's at about $110,000 right now. There hasn't been anybody that has garnered this much popularity in years."

"Enough!" the captain barked. He pointed a sharp finger at Whelan. "If I tell you to find him and arrest him, you'll do it."

Whelan walked from the office and slammed the door behind him. He was nobody's slave and saw no justice in arresting the savior of a female victim.

FOUR MONTHS LATER

Alvin, Texas, south of Pearland
Late January

Twenty-three-year-old Peyton Phoenix, once known only as *Jane Doe*, left the Pearland Medical Center and physical rehabilitation facility four months and two days after she was attacked, and went home. Her family hovered close by at all times, and 'Peyton' did her best to accept it. She thought it was cute but annoying. The apartment they set up for her was spartan, to say the least, but it was safe, and safe was enough.

"Mom, really, you don't have to finish those dishes," Peyton said. "Really, I've got it."

Peyton's mom turned around, wiping her hands with a dish towel. Her eyes were red; her cheeks, flushed.

"Oh, mom. I'm fine. I know you're worried about me, but I'll be all right."

"Promise me." Her mother was on the verge of tears again. "Promise me you'll stay clear of bad places."

"Mom, I was just living my life, and something bad happened. I went into that bar because, well, I don't know. I was curious, I guess." In reality, Peyton was more than curious about bikers. "I'm not going to let it ruin the rest of my life. I'm going to live it. I'm going to live my life." After a moment more of staring into her mother's sad eyes, Peyton said, "I promise," though she didn't know if she meant it.

Her mom took Peyton's face in her hands and studied her healing scars. "You know what I'm talking about," her mom said, still tilting Peyton's head from side to side. But Peyton just waited. "I'm talking about your outbursts."

"Oh, mother," Peyton said as she removed her mother's hands.

"No, I mean it. Peyton Phoenix, you listen to me." Her mother pointed a sharp finger at her. "You have a long way to go in this recovery. And there's anger brewing inside you. Maybe you don't see it, but I do. I've never seen such sudden, hidden rage. It scares me, honey." The South Texas drawl oozed out at the corners of her words. "You've always had a, well, a temper. But this. Honey, this is so unlike you."

"Well, mom, they raped me. They held me down and raped me. Sometimes it makes me so angry I don't know what I could do."

"That's exactly what I'm talking about. Honey, no one knows what you've been through other than you. But that rage, it will eat you alive. You've got to keep going back to the clinic for your appointments with the psychologist. She's there to help. Please let her. Do it for me?"

Peyton shook her head. She knew far more about her internal rage toward her attackers than she let on.

* * *

And so it was. Peyton Phoenix was independent once again. Peyton was a smart girl and not one easily fooled. She'd done well in college. Well, she'd done well once she had grown up a bit. But she hadn't exactly started out on the right foot. She'd had one semester at the University of Houston, and was midway through her second before being politely asked to leave. It wasn't her behavior that was at issue, they had said; it was her grades.

But Peyton knew better. It actually *was* her behavior that had led to the first demise of her life. Being kicked out of a prestigious university was a bitter disappointment, but she had no one to blame but herself. At U of H, the partying was good, but the frat boys were better.

Peyton didn't like to admit it and would be horrified if her mother ever found out, but back then Peyton had a wild streak in her. It was different from the temper flares that sometimes exploded out of her, seemingly out of nowhere. The sexual promiscuity was the kind of thing that many young coeds go through, but for Peyton, it had gone past the point of normalcy.

She had wanted to immerse herself in collegiate life right

from the start. She'd joined a sorority, and two months later, she knew she'd made a mistake. The girls were great, but the access to social life on campus that it afforded her was too much. Peyton was hooked on it.

She found out one thing about herself during that time—*she never knew exactly how far she'd go in a given situation.* It wasn't that she was out of control and would go on wild sexual binges. But within a week of being on campus, she knew it was time to satisfy a writhing curiosity.

She didn't even speak to the first guy she was with. They both had kept quiet, and no one at the party saw a thing. The rush, the danger, the thrill was intoxicating, and Peyton was addicted.

At the end of the semester, however, her joyride ended when her grades returned less than stellar results. She'd made all D's and one C. Her mother was in shock.

But, Peyton returned home to Alvin and decided to hold her head high. She applied for the summer semester at Alvin Community College, a school of around fifty-three hundred students. The college had been more than happy to give her a second chance at a degree.

When she left home for the second time, she thought the smaller setting would do her good. It was still just far enough away that Peyton could live in the dorm without fear of any surprise visits from her mother. This time, she had a better handle on what to expect, and how much work it would take to earn her way through.

Since there was no local chapter of her sorority, Peyton lived out those next college years as an 'independent,' a person without Greek affiliation. But that proved to be advantageous since she had no sorority functions to attend.

For a girl who, at the time, was interested in conquests at U of H, there had been another disadvantage. Pledging the sorority meant that they tended to only hang out with a few select fraternities on weekends. It wasn't such a bad thing, but there were so many other men out there, it seemed a shame. At ACC, Peyton circulated with the college's twenty-six hundred male students. Some were duds, of course, but for the most part, these guys knew how to party.

Physically, Peyton never had difficulty attracting attention. She had shiny, dark hair which framed eyes of deep brown. Yet she possessed a strange combination of a sweet-girl face, a petite frame, with a sneaking temper that brewed just beneath the surface. Keeping a low profile was the hard part. She didn't want people to know how many men she'd slept with. So, she'd go to class, study at the library for a few hours, and by nightfall, she'd go looking for a challenge. The easier ones were the guys she'd catch looking at her at a party. But they rarely provided her the risk she was looking for.

"What?" one boy with stark brown hair and thick eyebrows had said. "You want to go where?"

Peyton knew her exploits would get her in trouble one day, but the addiction was too strong. She persisted. "On the roof. Come on, take me up to the roof. I want to look at the stars."

"Are you crazy? Somebody will walk up there for sure. We go up to the roof of this library all the time."

"That's what makes it so *dangerous*," Peyton had giggled.

Peyton had her way with him, as she did with most men she wanted. And as time went by, the addiction increased. But as it did, Peyton's satisfaction with sneaking into someplace they weren't supposed to be became less satisfying. The cycle was closing in on her.

By the time she graduated, she had fallen into a rut and wanted out. She decided what she needed was fewer encounters, but encounters with more danger, more daring, and more risk.

And that's when it happened. Peyton walked into Chopper Town, a notoriously rough biker bar just ten miles to the north of her home. That night she had thrills on her mind. She had no idea that it could all go so wrong so fast. The Lincoln Killers were a ruthless gang, every one a hardened felon, and Peyton had become easy prey that night. If she'd have known who they were, she would have never gone in.

That night, Peyton had no intention, nor desire, to be attacked. She provoked no one. She may have had men on her brain when she went looking for a biker to hook up with, but what happened was not her fault, and she knew it.

And now, months after the attack, the little flame of underlying anger grew inside her. It was becoming a torrent that even she might not be able to control.

9

DREAMS

Bailey Bank and Trust, Alvin, Texas

Dreams came to Peyton in fits and starts. Some were nightmares, nightmares of that terrible night. During her waking hours, Peyton was blissfully unable to remember the details of the attack. But at night, the demons came. She would see herself in the back room of that cheap bar. The smell was etched onto her mind, like carvings in a statue. The memories were filled with the stench of bad body odor and stale beer. Just walking through the door of that place had been her only mistake. But then again, a woman should be able to go wherever she damn well pleases without being attacked. The rage grew inside her.

There were other dreams of the attack where she would see flashes of the face of the man who saved her. The concussion had removed most of her memory of the event, but his face would not budge. She knew it was a face that would forever dwell in the recesses of her mind. His jawline and high cheekbones were square and solid, like something cold-forged out of molten steel. His eyes, a piercing blue. And his hair, black, wavy and long. What stuck in her mind most was his rage. Watching him break bones and take down each biker one at a time was the most exhilarating thing she had ever seen.

Peyton sometimes dreamt the same dream, only, in this version, she was the one breaking the gang members into little pieces. The face of her rescuer that night was as rage-filled as she'd ever seen, yet there was a stoic control in it at the same time—a paradox she could not quite reconcile.

And then, she had memories of his face when she was in the hospital. It was the same face. He would visit her during the night. *But how could that be?* Peyton thought. *Maybe this is all just my imagination. I've been watching the coverage of my attack on the six o'clock news too much.* But the face was there. She was sure of it. What she remembered most about it from the hospital was his warmth, his caring. He was so devil-ishly good looking. This was not the face of a cold-blooded killer like they talked about on the news. This was the face of someone deeply committed to what he believed in.

Peyton stared at the computer monitor, then shook her head, trying to rock free of the distractions. Her new job as a loan officer at Bailey Bank and Trust was going well, and she didn't want to blow it.

"Miss Phoenix?" Mr. Lorrance, her boss, said. Lorrance

was an older man, a proper banker, but his bottom shirt button had broken loose under the strain of the spare tire it attempted to conceal.

"Huh? Oh, sorry, Mr. Lorrance. Yes, how can I help you?"

"This is Mr. Jenkins," Lorrance said. "He and his wife are looking at buying their first home. Can you walk him through our thirty-year fixed and variable rate mortgage products, please?"

"Oh, yes, sir. Nice to meet you Mr. Jenkins." Peyton rose to shake the man's hand.

Peyton had been caught daydreaming on the job again, and she knew it. Lorrance gave her a look of slight disapproval, but then smiled curtly and walked on.

Peyton talked for several minutes to the customer about the particulars of what types of loans were available. "And we also have a fifteen-year variable rate, it's tied to the LIBOR, but I won't bore you with the details of that. . ." Peyton's eyes drifted across the bank floor and out the ten-foot tall glass windows. Then, the expression on her face went blank.

"Miss Phoenix?" the customer said.

Peyton's eyes locked on a man walking on the sidewalk, and she followed him until he was just about to disappear from sight. *It's him!* she thought. *Oh, my God, it's him. And I thought it was all my imagination.*

"Miss Phoenix? Hello."

Peyton didn't hear any of it. The man walking on the sidewalk stopped, turned his head to look through the glass, and looked right at her. Peyton's mouth dropped open. Her vision became blurry, and when she looked again, he was gone.

"Are you okay?" the man at her desk said. "You look like you just saw a ghost."

"What? Oh, I think I did." She pasted a polite smile on her face, yet her heart raced. Suddenly, she became self-conscious that she was blushing.

10

WHELAN ON THE HUNT

Pearland Police Department

"Well, no, it's not going well at all," Lt. Whelan said as he stood in the captain's office doorway.

"And why not? I said I wanted this vigilante tracked down. Are you stalling?" the captain replied.

"Stalling? Are you out of your mind?" Whelan crossed his arms. "No, I'm not stalling."

"Good. Don't."

"It's just that I keep hitting brick walls. None of the witnesses at the bar that night had ever seen him before. And apparently, he didn't talk to anyone, not even the bartender."

"Oh, bullshit. He talked. Did you interview all the women in there?"

"Of course, I did. Several of them have distinct memories of him."

"What do they say?"

"Rough types, mostly. They said he was eye-candy, but kind of brooding, like somebody with a dark side. They wanted to get to know him better, a lot better if you know what I mean."

"And what about fingerprints? You know good and well he left prints all over that place."

Whelan stared at the captain a moment. "He did."

"And? What's the problem? Did you run the prints?"

"Of course, I ran the prints. What do you think I am, an idiot?"

"Watch it, jackass," the captain belted out as he pointed an angry finger at Whelan.

"Yes, I ran the prints, but when they came back—"

"No hit?"

"Oh, there was a hit all right. But they belonged to a dead guy."

"Come again?"

"I'm saying that our vigilante, the hero to women everywhere, is a ghost. Not literally, of course. These are definitely his fingerprints, but the identity tied to the fingerprints belong to a man named William Borders, deceased. Died two years ago this December. Chicago, Illinois, in a car accident."

"You mean to tell me he's stolen someone's identity? Dammit! But . . . even if he did steal an identity, stolen identities aren't tied to fingerprints. A stolen identity is tied to a Social Security number, then they get the credit cards, write a bunch of bad checks, take out a big fat loan and all that. There's no way his fingerprints would be changed in the system."

"There's one way they could be," Whelan said with a certain air of authority.

"Is that so?" the captain said with a smirk on his face. "Since you know so much, why don't you share your extensive knowledge with the rest of us?"

"He could be a spook."

"A spy? Bullshit."

"Think about it. We're talking ex-military, someone trained in close combat. Covert ops, CIA, or something like that. Did you see how he annihilated those bikers? And both you and I know that only the government would have access to change a person's fingerprints in the FBI's Automated Fingerprint Identification System.

"Whoever he is, he's highly trained. That much was obvious on the surveillance tapes. He's someone who's done this before, many times I'd say."

"Done what? Saved a woman from being attacked?"

"Killing. He's no virgin when it comes to killing people."

"And you're telling me that some ex-assassin, paramilitary guy, who kills for a living, has also got a soft spot in his heart for women? You're full of shit."

"That's exactly what I'm telling you," Whelan said. "And that's exactly what I put in my report to the Bureau."

"You sent a request for a psychological profile to the FBI? That kind of thing goes through my office first! You are out of line."

An awkward silence ensued.

The captain railed on. "And you told them he likely had a heart for women's rights, didn't you? You must be insane."

Whelan walked out but turned back. "And the FBI told me they've been looking for him for a long time. He's no ghost, captain. He's real." Whelan stormed out. He knew he had won the argument, but wondered if that was such a good idea in the first place. One thing was certain though. He knew he had better find this vigilante, and fast. His job depended on it.

11

RAGE

Alvin, Texas

Peyton sat up in bed, drenched in sweat. Her breathing was out of control and her heart rate erratic. She screamed into the tears that poured down her face. The nightmare, it was the nightmare. It was all so terrible. In the dream, Peyton had been catapulted back into that dark, horrific night when it happened.

The Lincoln Killers biker gang had nearly killed her that night. She could have died from the concussion alone. But that was something she didn't remember. It had been before they'd smashed her on the head with a bottle of Jim Beam that they'd choked her unconscious.

She couldn't breathe. The crushing forearm wrapped around her neck wrenched tighter and tighter, pinching off the blood supply to her brain and her windpipe. Now, in her own bedroom, she gasped for air and gripped at her throat.

"The bastards!" she yelled. "I swear. I'm going to kill them. I'm going to find the rest of them and kill them all." The tears roared forward but only served to strengthen her resolve.

* * *

Several hours later, the morning sun came through the windows with a brightness that help dissolve the earlier tension. Peyton thought back to her early days in college. Those were wild times. It was then that she had realized she no longer knew just how far she'd go in a given situation. Back then, she had taken on plenty of risks where sex was concerned. But now, instead of not knowing how far she'd go for a good time, this time she didn't know how far she'd go to get revenge.

Revenge was the only way, she'd convinced herself. *If they're all dead, the demons that come in my nightmares will stop. They'll stop and never come back.* At least, that was the lie she told herself.

In college, things had been much more straightforward. At that time, her life was a synchronized series of movements, each action intended to produce a particular outcome. She'd wake up early to get to class, study for several hours in the afternoon, then go out and do a little bit of what Peyton called 'scouting.' It wasn't a mission to locate the night's prey: the best-looking guy she could find.

Instead, what Peyton would look for was the next location she wanted the act to occur.

Although sex was the goal, finding that was easy. For Peyton, sexual gratification wasn't enough. She had wanted that extra layer of excitement—a place where someone could walk in on them at any moment. The hard part was finding a location that would provide the perfect balance of seclusion and danger. And the more danger, the better.

To her, the location was the one variable she could control. She favored places that were dangerously close to where people might walk by. She wanted to be close enough to hear their footsteps coming. It was a slippery slope and a game she played all too well. Convincing the guy to agree to the location was often another, more challenging matter.

But ever since all the awful things happened, Peyton felt robbed of such pleasures. The danger was no longer a turn-on, and Peyton didn't know how to restart her life. She didn't know how she'd feel if she found someone she cared about. And, she didn't know if she'd ever go back to genuinely feeling free. She believed she'd always feel threatened. But worst of all, she believed she would never be able to enjoy being with a man again without thinking about that night.

Peyton leaned into her pillow and cried until exhaustion took its toll and she drifted back to sleep.

12

HIM

His name was Brock Paladin. He was a bit of a free-thinking loner who had spent so much time living "under the radar" he no longer remembered what it meant to be "on the grid."

It was twelve years prior when he'd first been recruited by the CIA. At the time, he was finishing his undergraduate degree in forensic criminology at the University of Virginia. A man approached him. Perhaps it was the degree, the fact that Brock had scored off the charts on the GMAT exam, or something in his background that first alerted the CIA recruiter to seek Brock out. He appeared to be the perfect fit for the role of a covert operative. At any rate, Brock Paladin was literally hunted down by the Company, as the CIA is euphemistically known, and recruited into their training program.

The training was long and intense. Brock already had extensive experience in martial arts, his favorite sport during his teenage years, and that only accelerated his release into active duty.

Brock's upbringing, though, had been horrific. His father had been a raging alcoholic. He would come home drunk and beat Brock's mother. Brock spent most of his teenage years staying up late to await his father's arrival. He'd then provoke his father so that he'd come after him and not his mom. Even with the martial arts training, the results were never good. Brock wound up in the hospital more than once himself.

"You're ready now," his CIA trainer had finally said. "It's time for your first assignment. The targets you'll be handed are a clear and present danger to the national security of the United States. What you'll be doing is critical to the survival of our nation."

"No women," Brock had replied in a steady tone.

"What's that supposed to mean?"

"I'll serve my country. If assassination is what the country requires, that's what it will get. But no women. I'll not harm a woman."

The trainer jabbed a sharp finger into Brock's chest. "You'll do what you're ordered to do. You're not given the authority to make those determinations on your own."

"I'll only say it one more time. No women." It was an old-school pissing match, and Brock would not back down.

Growing up, watching his mother suffer, Brock developed a kind of bond—a kindred understanding between himself and certain women. Some women were what he thought of as vulnerable, at-risk. The ones he'd seen on the news that had been attacked or abused. Brock wouldn't tolerate it.

Over the years, he'd exacted revenge on men who deserved it. In fact, during his service to the CIA, he'd become distracted in his acts of protecting women so many times that he eventually was suspended from active duty. The sideshows were compromising the primary mission. After that, he'd resigned and gone to work with a splinter group comprised of private contractors. Different governments would hire them from time to time. As long as the morals were right, and the money was there, Brock had no problem with it.

He'd eventually accumulated enough cash to never really have to worry about it again, and that's when he decided to go off the grid. He'd assumed yet another identity, and just disappeared. Whether it was for God and country, or for money, he was done with killing.

But that was before he pulled his Harley Davidson Fatboy onto the dirt lot of a shit-hole bar named Chopper Town, and heard screams coming from the back room.

13

THE BANK

Bailey Bank and Trust, Alvin, Texas

The next morning, Peyton leaned against the counter in the bank's break room, sipping the below-average coffee.

"Girl, where are you?" Kiki, one of the tellers, said as she walked in. Kiki was a little taller and more stick-like than Peyton, yet the two shared similar features. Sometimes the bank manager got the two girls confused. Kiki's overuse of eye makeup though, made her look like a "trailer park" version of Peyton. "You sure aren't here. You look like you're off in your own world again."

Peyton looked up. "What? Oh, no, sorry. Daydreaming I guess."

Kiki grinned. "Uh huh. Daydreaming about that man again."

"Oh stop," Peyton said with a little grin.

"Tell me about him again? He sounds too good to be true. Let me see if I remember what you said. Dark wavy hair, dreamy blue eyes, shoulders out to here, a thin waist, and an ass made of steel."

Peyton burst out laughing. "Stop it. Kiki, you're too much."

"Why do you do this to yourself, child? You know he's not real. You said so yourself, like it was something out of a dream."

"He's real all right."

"When are you going to grow up?"

"I saw him."

"I know, Peyton, I know. You said you saw his face when he saved you, but no one else did. You said you saw him in the hospital, but no one else did. What now? Did he come to visit you in your bedroom last night?" Kiki giggled like a ten-year-old girl.

"No, I saw him. I saw him yesterday. Right outside the window. He walked by and stopped. Looked right at me. Kiki, my heart didn't just skip a beat, it stopped completely."

"Oooooh, child. You've got to get control of that imagination of yours."

"Kiki, he's real. I don't think I let myself believe that until yesterday. I mean, I know a real man saved me that night. But in all my memories of someone visiting me late at night in the hospital, he was so, so beautiful and kind. Like a protector, you know? It just seemed too good to be true." Peyton stared off into the corner of the room, lost in her own thoughts. Then, her tone changed. "A protector." She shook her head and took another sip of coffee. She winced against its scalding temperature. "A woman shouldn't need a protector." She looked at Kiki and gritted her teeth. "Sometimes I get so angry, I want to drive over to that bar and kill those sons of bitches."

"Good Lord, child. Hello in there," Kiki said as she waved her hand. It was a veiled attempt to distract Peyton from her state of anger. "Okay, so let's say he's real. What now? How are you going to meet him? What are you going to say to him? Are you going to just jump his bones or what?" Kiki laughed.

"It's not all about getting a man into bed, Kiki."

"Yeah, right."

"Well, anyway, I can't stop thinking about him. I mean, he's real, Kiki, he's real. And oh my God, he's so, so . . . I don't know. He means so much to me, and I don't even know him. I don't even know his name."

Kiki crossed her arms. "That detective that keeps coming by here seems to know something, that's for sure. What are you going to do about that? You know the police are looking for this guy. You need to get over him, you hear me? Peyton Phoenix, girl, you look at me. How are you going to get over him?"

Peyton slid her head back and cast Kiki a sultry grin. "I'm not going to get over him. I'm going to get under him."

They both knew she was joking, but nonetheless, the two erupted into laughter loud enough to cause others in the typically quiet bank building to hear.

14

SURVEILLANCE

The sidewalk in the tiny downtown area was typically quiet. It was only at lunchtime that it became cluttered, and today was no different. People on both sides of the sidewalk emerged from their various places of business and walked in different directions, some of them stopping at a diner on the corner.

But Brock would take no such luxury. He was here for a purpose, a purpose he hoped would be unnecessary. Brock had had a bad feeling of late. It was a feeling deep in the pit of his gut that told him, somehow, that the woman he saved, Peyton Phoenix, was not safe. The trial of the surviving Lincoln Killer gang member was not far off, and Brock knew any witnesses to the event would be targets. In his way of thinking, it was all too obvious that Peyton would be target number one.

Brock had been on missions all over the world, and one

thing rang true: thugs were thugs no matter where you went. There was a consistency in their thinking. It didn't matter that one gang spoke English, another Mandarin, and a third, a Chechnyan dialect of Russian. They all thought the same way. It was a simple process—one in which they felt completely justified in killing anyone who got in their way. The systematic murder or intimidation of witnesses was the same all over the world.

Brock stood on the sidewalk and leaned against an empty storefront diagonal to the bank and watched Peyton through the glass for a few moments. Not wanting to attract attention, he turned and walked down the street until he found the alleyway. Once behind the vacant storefront, his training kicked in. He pulled some small tools from underneath his thick leather belt and inserted them into the lock. The lock was probably installed in the 1970s; it only took him a moment to pick it.

Once inside, he looked at the open expanse. Large, hand-cut hardwood planks lined the floor, a telltale sign that the building had originally been built decades before the 1970s.

He walked across the creaking planks until he found what he was looking for—a staircase to the second floor. Once upstairs, he walked to an old sliding window at the back that led onto the rusty metal fire escape. He unclasped the window lock and yanked against it to pull it open. It was stuck, but as he slammed his hand into the casing, the window came free. He crawled out onto the metal platform. From there, his ascent to the roof was as simple as standing on top of the railing, then pulling himself up.

He walked across the tarred roof until he was at the front of the building.

The rooftop afforded him a better view of the streets below. He could see quite a distance in either direction. And since he was able to stay hidden behind a small, rotting billboard, no one would notice his presence.

Brock had done surveillance on countless missions. It was a staple of the trade. Get yourself in a position where no one can see you, and watch as the action unfolds. His presence on the rooftop hideout today was no different than any day of the past two weeks. He had sat and watched from similar locations hoping beyond hope to not see anything that would alarm him.

But then it happened. At about two in the afternoon, two chopper-style motorbikes rumbled off a side street and slowly cruised in front of the bank. The riders looked like hardened thugs. Leather vests adorned with gang colors, torn jeans, dew rags on their heads, and thick dark sunglasses.

As they cruised in front of the bank, they slowed, and Brock couldn't help but notice the somewhat obvious turn of each of their heads. They were casing the joint.

For just a moment, Brock allowed himself to think that perhaps their only intention was to rob the bank. But as his eyes followed them through a pair of miniaturized binoculars, he could read the large leather patches on their backs. The patches simply said, *Lincoln Killers*. They weren't going to rob the bank, they were going to kill Peyton Phoenix.

He watched as they accelerated down the street. He shook his head and said to himself, "I hate it when I'm right."

Brock stood, walked across the rooftop and descended back down the building. He knew he would have to act, and the time was near.

15

OFF THE GRID

Brock's experience told him it was dangerous to hang around town, but he just couldn't bring himself to leave. Cops were everywhere. The incident at the biker bar had garnered national news, and now, the cops wanted an arrest.

But today, sitting in his apartment, he spoke to himself. "Why do they care that I killed those assholes? The girl needed help, and I helped her." Seeing that poor girl attacked brought up repressed feelings that he'd thought were long buried. But what scared him more was the unexpected knock on the door. Brock jumped up and yanked a Glock from his waistband.

Who the hell is that? he thought. *No one even knows who I am, much less where I live.*

"Come on, compadre," a raspy, guttural voice said from the other side of the door. "I know you're in there. Open the damn door and get me a beer already."

"Will?" Brock said as he peered through the peephole.

"Yes, you big baby," Will replied. "Now put that Glock away and open the door. I know you're holding it."

When the door opened, Brock smiled. "Holy shit, Will! Damn, I never thought I'd see you this far east. Come on in."

The two men embraced and gave each other a prototypical male chuck on the back.

"Damn," Will said. "It's been a long time."

"You look like shit," Brock said as he stepped back and laughed. "Look at you. Five days of gray stubble, your hair all long. Hell, the last time we worked together you had a shaved head. Maybe that's why I didn't notice all the gray."

"Gray, huh?" Will said. "And you, you young pissant. Look at you. What the hell is this? All leathered up? You *look* like a biker, all right. Is this what you always wanted to be? A biker? And you're telling me *my* hair is long? You look like you sing lead for a big-haired '80s band."

"Oh, shut up. Let me get you a beer. Your favorite."

"Shit, I'll bet all you've got in there is Pabst Blue Ribbon. Is that all you ever drink?"

Brock walked to the refrigerator.

"Hey, Will," he called, "you remember that shithole in Bangkok? We got into that fight with that little dude with the shiny green suit?"

"Remember it? We were so drunk we nearly got our asses kicked by that little pipsqueak."

Brock handed Will a beer.

Will popped the cap and held it high. "To old friends."

"Best friends," Brock said as he clinked his beer can into Will's.

"I come all the way across the country to see you, and all you have to offer me is a warm PBR. Man, times haven't changed."

Brock crossed his arms. "How the hell did you find me anyway? Scared the shit out of me when you knocked on the door. No one knows I'm here. I was about to go all postal on your ass."

Will was a good twenty years Brock's senior and had always been a mentor to Brock. That role was not about to end now. "Uh huh. What would you have to be so scared about with someone knocking on your door? Hmm, compadre?"

Brock looked down and exhaled. His lack of words and stoic expression spoke volumes.

Will set his beer on the coffee table. "Got yourself in deep kimchi now, haven't you?"

"What are you talking about?"

"What am I talking about? It's me you're talking to, man. It's all over the news, even out on the beaches in sunny California, where I'd rather be right now, by the way."

"Typical Will. Always on the beach." Brock asked.

"Warm sun, warm girls. What not to love about that? But," Will took a long swig of beer, "when I saw the news footage from that biker bar, I knew it was you. They keep playing a tiny clip of the surveillance tape. Didn't take me a second to recognize you."

"My face isn't even visible in that."

"It's your style, compadre. The way you move. Hell, I taught you half that shit as it is. Now, I just have one question for you: why are you still in this crappy little town? Man, you should have hopped on that Fatboy and blown clear of this place the moment the fight was over."

"I couldn't. I couldn't leave," Brock replied.

Will looked at Brock out of the side of his eye. His facial expression was akin to one who's just watched his puppy shat on the rug. "I can read you like a book, compadre." Will shook his head. Referring to an incident in Brock's past, he said, "You're still carrying that shit around with you, aren't you? Dammit, I thought you were through with all that."

Brock could not avert his eyes from the carpet.

Will poked a sharp finger into Brock's shoulder. "That girl died ten damn years ago, man. And ten thousand miles from here. There wasn't a thing you could have done about it. That guy had it in for you. And she just got in the way, that's all."

Brock flung his beer can into the wall and lunged at Will. "You leave Lori out of it!"

But Will spun him off. "I'm not the enemy, goddammit! But I tell you who is, it's you. Yeah, it's inside you, and you can't let it go. You chickenshit!" Will screamed. "I've told you a hundred times. Lori's death was not your fault. How could you know she would come home right after that mutherfucker broke into your place? He came there to kill you, and you know it. She was just in the wrong place at the wrong time." His volume trailed off. "And stop acting like it's just you who lost something. I loved her too, man. I loved Lori like a little sister."

The two exchanged hard glances.

"I should have been there," Brock said.

"You don't think I think about that too? I've gone over it in my head a hundred times. We had no way of knowing Pyongyang would send someone to kill you. If we had, we would have been there." Will pulled his long graying hair out of his eyes. "If I could give anything, just to stop him from raping and killing her, I'd give it. And look at you now. You walk into a biker bar, see the same thing happening to some chick you don't even know, and you go apeshit."

"I just—"

"You lost it is what you did. After seeing the clip of the surveillance tape on the news, I called a friend at the Bureau. He sent me the rest of the tape. Have you seen it?"

"No," Brock said as he looked down.

"Well, don't. What they did to that girl was . . . but the point is *you*. You didn't just pull them off of her, did you? Hell no. You methodically took them down, one by one. It was like shooting clays. More broken bones in that biker bar than in a graveyard. And after they were down and out of the fight, you went one by one, snapping their necks. I suppose the three bikers that lived long enough to ride to the hospital fooled you into thinking they were already dead. Am I right?"

Brock had no response.

"Come on, man," Will said. "Pack a bag. Let's get out of

this town and head up to the cabin. They're looking for you, compadre. And they won't stop until they find you."

"I'm off the grid. They'll never find me."

"*I* found you," Will said as he pointed to his chest.

"I can't leave, man. I can't."

"And why the hell not?"

"The girl. She's still here. I can't leave her. She's vulnerable."

"She's vulnerable." It was a statement carved in disgust, thick and pure. "And you think that if you save this girl, everything will be all right again? Losing Lori will be made okay? Is that what you think?"

"I don't know, man."

"Let me ask you something. Late at night, when the demons come, they look like Lori, don't they? Look me in the eye and tell me I'm wrong! And if you save this new girl, you think the demons will finally stop coming? Damn, you're a piece of work, compadre."

16

COMPADRES WITH A PLAN

"So why is it you say the girl is still vulnerable?" Will asked. "You saved her already, okay? That biker gang, what's their stupid name, the Lincoln Killers? Well, if the ones who are still alive have any sense, they'll stay away from both you and the girl."

"They're watching her," Brock replied.

"You're paranoid."

"I follow them sometimes. They drive by the bank where she works. I watch her from a building across the street. They'll come for her. At some point, they'll come for her, and I'm going to be there when they do."

Will was incredulous. "Why in the hell would they be after her? It makes no sense. Half their gang already raped her and beat her half to death. She'd be dead right now if it wasn't for you." He got up and began pacing. "If they're mad at anybody, it's you."

"I haven't figured that out yet."

After walking the main room of the apartment several times, Will stopped and looked out the sliding glass doors. "I knew you were going to drag me into another one of your fucking causes. What do we need to do?"

"You'll help me?" Brock said, staring at his beer.

Will turned on him. "I can't believe you just said that. After all, we've been through? After you pulled my ass out of the sling in Croatia, and that time in Kandahar, and a half dozen other times? Maybe I was your mentor in those days, but you saved my ass more than once. We're blood. You understand me, compadre? We're blood."

Brock knew Will was right. They'd been in more bad shit than he could recall, and Will was always there for him. Brock nodded.

Will asked, "If they're tracking her, they're going to have to be taken out, aren't they? The Lincoln Killers."

"I don't see another way. They're a bunch of lowlifes. I doubt they even know how to change their minds once they're made up. They're going to kill her all right."

"She's got to be told, man. You've got to tell her the danger she's in."

"I've been thinking the same thing," Brock said through a long exhale.

"Before we do this, I want you to look at me. Look me in the eye."

Brock complied.

Will studied Brock a moment, then shook his head. "Shit, you've fallen for this girl, haven't you?"

There was a long pause, and Brock struggled to maintain eye contact with his mentor. "I don't know what you're talking about."

"Cut the bullshit."

Brock's shoulders slumped. "I don't know how it happened."

Will paced across the carpeted apartment floor. "Goddammit, I knew it. This chick reminds you of Lori, doesn't she? And now you've fallen for her. Do you even know her? Hell, she could be a nut job."

"I know, I know. It just snuck up on me," Brock said.

"In love with a girl you don't even know. And she's at least ten years younger than your sorry ass."

"I'm not *in love* with her, all right?"

Will laughed. "You are such a pussy, you know that? Well, this ups the stakes. The fact that you've got the hots for this chick means your ability to think critically is compromised."

"Oh, come on. I can still think clearly in a combat situation."

"Oh really? Thinking clearly? Like you were thinking clearly when you snapped four of those biker's necks after you'd already taken them out of commission? Is that the clear thinking you're talking about?" Will shook his head. "No, you've got to get control of that, compadre. If we're going to do this thing, you've got to quit thinking with your dick."

"Hey!" Brock barked. "This girl is not just someone to have sex with. She deserves better than that. And after what happened to her, it wouldn't surprise me if she never wanted to have sex again. And I wouldn't blame her. But, it doesn't change my feelings."

Will walked up to Brock and stood six inches from his face. "You've changed, man. Maybe you're finally growing up."

"Oh, fuck you," Brock said as he shoved Will back. "Growing up, huh? All right there, *dad*. You got any ideas for this grown-up?"

"Yeah, you quit being such a dumbass. The Lincoln Killers don't have to be taken out. We bring the girl in. We hide her. We can't risk her being out in the open like this. She'll just disappear. After that, she needs to know how to protect herself."

"Train her?"

"Damn right."

17

BUREAU

FBI Field Office, Texas City

Whelan slammed his desk phone down. "Dammit!" he said.

A uniformed officer walking past smiled then said, "What's the matter, Lieutenant? Your mama can't come over for supper tonight?" The man laughed and continued walking.

"Kiss my ass," Whelan said, though he knew the officer was joking. He had just tried for the third time to get the FBI to give him a straight answer. Had they completed the psychological profile of the Terminator or not? Whelan didn't know what the delay was down at the FBI field office, but whatever was happening down there, they were stalling.

Whelan stood and grabbed his coat jacket. Moments later he was in his undercover cruiser. He inserted the keys, and the Crown Vic surged to life. He backed up then headed out to catch the Sam Houston Tollway east to I-45 south and then on to Texas City. The field office was a three-story, unmarked glass-and-brick building, not large, but it served its purpose. He slid his badge around to the front of his belt, then walked inside.

The lobby area was small. A receptionist, seated behind a large pane of bulletproof glass, smiled. He walked to the window. She glanced at his badge then spoke into a mic, "Can I help you?"

"Lieutenant Dan Whelan. I need to see Special Agent Wilmont. Can you tell him I'm here?"

"Certainly, Lieutenant," she said. She keyed a few buttons into her phone then spoke into her headset. Being separated by two-inch thick glass, Whelan couldn't hear what she said.

But a few minutes later, a hardened steel door opened. "Whelan?" a man in a crisp white shirt and a red tie said. "Special Agent Stephen Wilmont," he said as he extended his hand. The two men shook. Wilmont let out a long exhale. "Come on back."

As the steel door slammed shut, Whelan noticed that the federal office space looked no different than any other— floors covered with industrial carpet, individual offices on one side and a cube farm in the center. He followed Agent Wilmont into an office and took a seat in front of the man's desk. Wilmont closed the door and sat in his desk chair. He leaned his elbows onto the desk and interlocked his fingers. "What brings you in, Lieutenant?" the agent said.

"You know exactly what brings me down here. You're

stalling on the psychological profile of the Terminator. I've got multiple homicides to investigate, and I want that profile."

"The FBI is not beholden to local law enforcement."

"I didn't say you were. I simply said you were stalling, and I want to know why."

When Special Agent Wilmont did not answer, Whelan leaned forward in his chair.

"Listen, you know full well that some guy walked into a bar and stopped a brutal attack on a female victim. He killed seven men in the process. The trial of the one survivor comes up in a few weeks. We're talking about a young woman's life here. She barely survived, and I wouldn't doubt if she's in danger now. We need every bit of help we can get. We need to find this man. He may be guilty of going too far, but if we don't find him before the Lincoln Killers gang does, he'll be dead too."

Wilmont leaned back. "You admire him, don't you?"

"Since this murder is a state crime and not a federal one, you probably didn't look at the rap sheets of these thugs that he killed."

Wilmont smiled. "I did look at them. And between you and me, I kind of admire this Terminator son of a bitch myself."

Whelan sat back. "Then why are you stalling on the profile?"

Wilmont lowered his voice. "This conversation does not leave this room. Am I understood?" Whelan nodded. "We're not stalling on the profile. The profile has been run."

"And?" Whelan asked.

"We got a match. The thing is, he's got a bit of a history, if you know what I mean."

"No, I don't."

"The Terminator was a wet boy."

Whelan closed his eyes as the thought played forward in his mind. "He was an assassin? That's what you're saying, isn't it?"

Special Agent Wilmont smiled. "No, I'm not saying anything at all. I have no comment, remember?"

"I need a name."

"No can do," Wilmont replied.

Whelan stood and extended a hand. He knew he had gotten more information than he should have. "I appreciate you *not* sharing anything with me." He smiled knowing full well the information he had obtained was quite valuable.

"Sorry I couldn't do more. Good luck to you, Lieutenant. But I hope you don't catch him."

As Whelan stepped into the hallway, he turned back and said, "Me neither."

18

VISIT FROM A FRIEND

Bailey Bank and Trust, Alvin, Texas

Peyton leaned an elbow on her office desk and daydreamed about meeting the man who'd saved her. He was no fantasy; he was real, and she knew it. Peyton couldn't stop herself from thinking about him.

"Girl, you better snap out of it before Mr. Lorrance catches you again," Kiki said. "Besides, you've got a customer waiting."

The man that stood before her was dressed in rough blue jeans, a sleeveless t-shirt, and leather vest. He looked like he'd just been dropped out of a movie set where they were filming a low-budget biker flick.

"Oh, yes sir. How can I help you?" Peyton cleared her throat and cast a nervous glance at Kiki.

"My name's Will," he said, removing his thick black sunglasses. "Wanted to get some information about a mortgage. Got my eyes on a little place up town." His salt-and-pepper hair was in stark contrast to the darkness of his eyes.

"Please, have a seat," Peyton said. "We have several thirty-year fixed mortgage products, as well as some with variable rates. Do you know what you had in mind?"

Will looked at Kiki who was studying him the way a person might study a predator. When Will's eyes met hers, she looked back to her computer monitor and resumed typing.

"You are in danger," he mouthed to Peyton. The statement startled her. Then he continued at normal volume, "The house I'm looking at buying is $145,000. I was thinking about putting twenty percent down." He looked at her with cold seriousness. But for some reason, to Peyton, his eyes were disarming. Looking at them instilled a kind of trust Peyton was not accustomed to.

"Ahem. Well," Peyton said, "you might consider a fifteen-year variable. The rates are at their lowest in years."

Will slipped a sealed envelope onto her desk, tucked it just underneath some other papers, then said, "And how much can the interest rate change in a given year?"

"What is this?" Peyton whispered. But before he could answer, she saw what was written on it. On the outside of the envelope, written in pencil, was one word.

Terminator

It was the same name used by news outlets across the country to refer to the man who had rescued her. Peyton swallowed hard. The man in front of her was certainly not the man that saved her. But, she continued:

"Rates can only increase by one and a half percent per year." Her voice cracked. "And you're guaranteed a cap of three-point-five percent." Peyton again whispered, "What is this envelope? What are you talking about?"

"That's very interesting. I've got another appointment," Will said. "I've got to get going, but I'd like to fill out a mortgage application. Can I take the paperwork with me?"

"Certainly. Here's a pre-approval packet, and my business card. Please let me know if you have any questions. My mobile number is on the card. And thanks for giving Bailey Bank and Trust a chance to earn your business."

He was gone as quickly as he had arrived. Peyton stared at the envelope, then quickly slid it into her desk drawer.

* * *

As the morning hours ticked by, Peyton stared at the top drawer of her desk. She wanted to rip that envelope open and see what was inside so badly that she could almost taste the envelope adhesive in her mouth. But thoughts bounced from one side of her head to the other. *Who was he? Am I really in danger? How can I trust him*? And worse, her nerves were beginning to fray. Every time the brass-framed glass door of the bank swung open, her head snapped in that direction. Fear was taking a not-so-subtle hold.

At last, the noon hour was upon her. Peyton jammed the envelope into her purse and was out the door before Kiki even had a chance to finish with a customer.

Walking out into the stark sunlight was almost eerie. The sharp light cast a blinding glaze across everything. It was so bright it reminded her of the first time she'd ever had an eye exam, and the optometrist had dilated her pupils.

Peyton ducked into a restaurant called The Corner Deli, a little hole-in-the-wall favored by the locals and took a seat. She pulled out the envelope. It felt like lead in her hands. Her apprehension was so high, she almost didn't have the nerve to open it.

She turned the envelope over and looked at it. It was a standard white envelope, the kind used in every business office in the country. The word 'Terminator' was hand-written in pale pencil and thus was very hard to see. She slipped her finger under the seal and started to put pressure against it.

"Have we decided?" a bubbly waitress with bright red hair said.

"Oh," Peyton said as she put a hand across her heart. "Sorry, you scared me."

"I'm sorry, honey. You take your time."

"No, no. I'll have the chicken-over-greens salad. Baked chicken, please."

"Be right out for you, hon."

The waitress disappeared. Peyton took a deep breath and tore into it.

Inside was a note on plain white paper. Taped to the paper was a single, silver key stamped with the numbers '2289.' The handwriting on the letter matched the outside of the envelope. It was written in a man's hand but was strangely neat and orderly.

"Peyton,

"My name is not important right now, but you must trust me. I am the one the news media calls The Terminator. I was there that night, that awful night at Chopper Town. You have to believe me when I tell you that I had just arrived, and from the first moment I heard screams, I went to help. I am sorry I was not there sooner. I lie awake at night wondering why I couldn't have gotten there earlier. If I had, I could have spared you a terrible ordeal.

"At any rate, your life is again in danger. The same biker gang, The Lincoln Killers, has been watching you. Please, I know you have no reason to believe me, but you are in danger. Do not return to your office. Do not return to your apartment. Turn off your cell phone. Go to the bus station that's two blocks south of the bank. Make sure no one is following you. Use the key to unlock locker number 2289. Inside you'll find proof of who I say I am, along with further instructions."

The note was not signed. Peyton sat in stunned silence. She looked around at each person in the deli with a profound sense of paranoia. "I'm in danger?" she said to herself. She ran her fingers across the key and stared out the large glass window. After a moment, she stood, then walked out the door.

19

THE SETUP

Super Pump Six gas station. About two miles west of Sand Mill, Arizona.

The Lincoln Killers gang left California with their leader, Grinder, in front on I-5 headed south. They'd decided to avoid Los Angeles – too many cops, and too many rival gangs – so they took I-40 through Bakersfield and picked up Highway 93 south toward Phoenix through a desolate section of Southern Arizona. They planned to pick up I-10 at Phoenix and ride it all the way to Houston.

As they approached a decrepit gas station on the outskirts of the town of Sand Mill on 93, Grinder put his hand into the air and waved it in a circle. It was the signal they were about to pull over. Loud Harleys of various models rumbled into the gas station and swarmed the pumps.

The owner of the station, an old man of about seventy-five years, put his hands on the arms of a creaky, wooden rocking chair where he was seated and pushed himself upright. He surveyed the group. He knew they looked like trouble but had no choice but to serve them.

The old man walked with a slight hunch. He approached Grinder and said, "Hep you?"

Grinder barely looked up. "Fill her up. In fact, fill them all up."

The man looked across the rough group of bikers then back at Grinder. He swallowed. "This be cash or charge?"

"We got money, old man." Grinder said. "We've always got money."

The old-timer nodded and went to a pump and began his work.

Grinder stood and arched his back. He walked around the side of the gas station building followed by his enforcer, Paul "Gears" Pliskin. When they were both outside of earshot of the others, Grinder said, "You sure we got this thing in the bag?"

"It won't be a problem, boss," Gears replied. "The bitch is predictable as hell. We've got her apartment address, we know her patterns, and get this, she works at a bank."

"So?"

"Don't you get it, boss? It's perfect. I've put the boys into motion already. They're going to make it look like a bank robbery gone bad. They'll charge in there wearing masks and rob the place. They'll shoot her in the process."

Grinder chuckled. "That's pretty good. Who you got on it? I sure as hell hope you didn't trust this to our local patches there. They've screwed too much of this up already."

Gears smirked. "No, I sent three of our boys out there a week ago. All three of them are hang-arounds, still hoping to earn their patch someday. They've all proven themselves in other work, and, so far as I can tell, they've done a pretty good job of surveillance on this bitch. When they told me where she worked, I sent in a specialist to join them."

"A bank specialist?" Grinder asked. "You sent in Lucifer, didn't you?"

"John 'Lucifer' Torrance. Did twelve bank jobs before doing ten long at San Quentin. He's been a patch of ours the last four years. Knows his way around a bank like nobody else. And we've got an added bonus this time."

"What's that?"

Gears replied, "All three hang–arounds are eager to earn their patch. One in particular. Hell, that kid would go after the president of the United States if we asked him to. Since you have to commit murder to earn your patch in the first place, this will be his big chance."

Grinder pulled off his dark sunglasses and shoved them onto the top of his head. "Just as long as he keeps his cool. We don't need any hotheads. Hell, committing murder inside a bank robbery is bad enough. It will bring down heat. But some gung-ho kid goes off half-cocked and kills a couple more, we'll have a bigger problem on our hands. Just make sure they know they're there to kill just one cunt to prevent her from testifying against us. Now, how are they going to keep from being identified?"

"Lucifer is in charge," Gears said. "He could do this blind-folded. They'll take off their colors, cover their faces, cover their arms so their tats can't be seen. They'll use shotguns so there won't be any ballistics to trace down the origin of the guns. Lucifer is on it. Piece of cake."

Grinder poked a stiffened finger into Gears' chest. "This had better work. I hold you personally responsible." He walked back to his Harley.

Gears exhaled. "Another day, another death threat."

A commotion at the pumps drew their attention. One of the patches had shoved the old man to the ground.

"What's this about?" Grinder shouted.

"The old fool spilled gas on my seat," the biker said.

"Serves him right, then," Gears growled.

Minutes later, as the elderly attendant nursed his bruised arm, the gang roared away toward Phoenix.

But the incident would have dire consequences. The old man called the Yavapai County Sheriff's Office to report the incident. The Lincoln Killers found themselves the subject of a statewide BOLO, or Be On The Lookout. They spent a week dodging patrols and finally had to hole up outside of Tucson until the heat was off. They wouldn't make it to Pearland until early February.

20

THE LOCKER

Bus Station, Alvin, Texas

Peyton walked down a few blocks, crossed the street of the tiny downtown area, and stood on the sidewalk, staring at her own reflection in the glass of the city's new bus station entrance. She reached out to grab the door handle but pulled her hand back as though afraid it might be hot to the touch. The door burst open, and a man popped out, nearly knocking into her.

"Oh, excuse me," the man said, shuffling past.

Peyton clutched her purse to her chest. Her breathing was erratic. *Calm down. My God, calm down,* she thought. Peyton paused a moment, then went inside and scanned the wide-open area looking for any signs of irregularity. She'd never been inside, and found the terminal larger than she'd thought.

The floor was gray-colored tile, polished to a high shine. Brilliant light shone off it from the long glass wall on the opposite side. She spotted the rows of rental lockers and walked toward them. When she saw the metal nameplate stamped 2289, she froze in her tracks. It was as if she was afraid a rattlesnake might be inside it. She checked and rechecked the number on her key. It was correct, and after a few final glances over her shoulder, she inserted the key into the lock. She turned it, and the locker popped open.

Inside was a long, white, paperboard box, the kind she'd seen a hundred times at the department store. Peyton pried open the front and peered inside. When she removed the top, she found a set of blue-green surgical scrubs, a surgical cap, booties for shoes, a stethoscope, and a hospital identification card. Each garment had been ironed, neatly pressed into fine creases, and placed inside the box with the precision of a military footlocker.

"Holy shit," she said as she looked at the identification card. "It's him. It's really him. He *did* visit me in the hospital." Peyton's heart fluttered. "Now what?"

A cell phone rang, and Peyton reached into her purse and pulled hers out. But the screen was black, and she realized she'd already turned it off, as instructed. The sound was instead coming from inside the locker—a phone was tucked underneath the surgical scrubs.

"Hello?" she said into the phone, her voice shaking.

"In the box, you'll find a bus ticket." The husky voice

was familiar, like something out of a dream. "Board the bus and sit in the second to the last row. Do it now."

The call went dead.

Peyton spun around and studied the people inside the terminal. She was frightened, but the more she thought about it, the more she determined herself she was doing the right thing. It was the voice. The voice was so calming and familiar. It was him.

She made for the other side of the terminal and went out the glass doors toward the boarding area. She was sure of only one thing: this person meant her no harm.

21

STITCHING THE SOUL

The bus was nearly empty as she stepped aboard. The driver held out his hand. "This is number two seventy-seven, to Galveston."

"Yes, thank you," Peyton said as she displayed her ticket.

She studied the few faces as she shuffled down the narrow aisle, looking for anything familiar. The smell on the bus invoked memories of her high school locker room. As she took her seat, in the second to the last row, the bus driver called out to the platform. "Number two seventy-seven, Galveston. Departs in one minute."

Peyton began to worry. Perhaps he wasn't coming. As the bus engine started and began to pull out, her heart sank. But ten minutes later, a husky voice from behind her whispered. It came from in between her seat and the empty one next to her.

"Don't turn around. Just keep looking forward," the voice

said. "You're safe. No one followed you aboard, but we can't be sure no one is following the bus. In about thirty minutes, the bus will pull in to its next stop. There's a Waffle House diner right near the station, just south on 61st Street near the seawall. Get off and walk toward the diner. Bring your things. You won't be getting back on the bus."

Peyton's heart raced. It was him. It was him, without a doubt. She so badly wanted to turn around. It was all so exciting, terrifying, and exhilarating all at the same time.

The minutes ticked by and all she could think about was what it would be like to stare at him. The visions of what he had looked like flickered in her mind's eye. The hair, so dark, wavy, and thick. And his arms. When he would visit late at night, the only thing exposed under his hospital scrubs were his forearms. Yet they were so muscular.

If it hadn't been for the man now seated behind her, she'd certainly be dead. Her mind raced in fits and starts. It surprised her that she had gone through with it and boarded the bus in the first place. Yet here she sat, on a bus headed into uncertainty with a man that she didn't even know.

He was almost too good to be true. Peyton knew this was more than a tough guy. He'd walked into Chopper Town alone that night and had taken on eight of the roughest bikers around, and won. There was something more than tough about him. It was like he was made of steel.

As the bus rocked gently back and forth down I-45, Peyton tried to not let her mind wander too far.

She recovered from the daydream as the bus pulled into the station. She gathered her things, stood and walked with the other passengers to the front of the bus, then stepped down, and began walking south toward the Waffle House. Just out of sight, as she continued in that direction, the man stepped down and walked to an adjacent parking lot where he had stored his Harley.

Just before Peyton got to the diner, the man pulled the motorcycle into her path. He was wearing a full helmet with a dark black cover. The cover completely obscured his face. He wore a white undershirt. His bare arms were well shaped, cut and lean. Several tattoos were woven across the broad span of his upper arms on either side, and long, wavy black hair jutted out from underneath his helmet. Peyton knew it was him.

She boarded the chopper without hesitation, slipped her petite arms around his waist, and held on as the acceleration of the bike intensified. She pulled herself tight against his V-shaped torso and closed her eyes. As the vibration of the bike accelerated south past the Waffle House, she drank in the smell of his hair.

A minute later, the bike pulled onto Seawall Boulevard and drove about three miles southwest to a place called The Dellanera RV Park. Just past a small tidal pond, a white RV sat in a parking lot.

The bike pulled behind it, and the driver expertly parked the bike on the trailer mounted to the back of the RV. When the engine stopped, Peyton wasn't sure if she should be scared or excited.

"You're safe," he said through the face mask. "I'm so glad

you came along." They both disembarked, and he removed his helmet.

There, Peyton stood face to face with the one man responsible for saving her life. He was even better looking than she had envisioned. The eyes were such a deep cobalt blue that she became lost in them.

"Tell me your name," Peyton said in a meek voice as she let her eyes wander down his chest.

"Brock. Brock Paladin."

"I don't know how to thank you for saving my life. That night was so horrible. I knew I was dead for sure. But then it all stopped, and when I looked back, you were . . . stopping them from hurting me any more. After that I blacked out."

"That's all behind us now. After it was over, I carried you out of there and draped you across my lap on the Harley and took you to the hospital."

"That was you sitting behind me on the bus?" She glanced at his bike. "Where did the bike come from?"

"I parked it here earlier then took the bus into Alvin. Come on, let's get inside the RV, we don't want to stay out in the open too long."

As they boarded, Peyton asked, "Why do you think I'm in danger?" She couldn't help but watch his walk as she followed him.

"This is my partner," Brock said as he pointed to Will.

Will nodded.

Peyton was a bit startled to see another man in the RV but immediately recognized him from his visit to her desk at the bank. She decided that if Brock trusted him, she should too. And even if she didn't, it was too late now.

To her, Will looked like a much older version of Brock. The hair was long and gray. He too could easily fit in at a biker bar. His skin looked like toughened leather that had been drug over concrete. But even so, he was not a bad looking man.

As Will started the RV's engine, Peyton sat on a bench seat. There were cracks in the vinyl upholstery. "Where are we going?"

Will replied, "We're headed down the coast a bit."

"Why? What are we going to do there?"

"Like my compadre said, little lady. You are in danger. So, first thing's first. We're getting you the hell out of here, and when we get where we're going, we're going to teach you how to defend yourself."

"Really?" Peyton looked at the two but had a hard time peeling her eyes away from Brock. "Do you really think I'm in danger? Let's start at the beginning. *Why* is it you think I'm in danger?"

"Not me, little lady," Will said "Him. He's the one that's dragged me into this little escapade."

Brock spoke, this time with a certain resignation in his tone. "I've been following some of the Lincoln Killers gang, tailing them. On several occasions in the last week, they've come by your bank. You're being followed."

"Following me?" Peyton's voice cracked. "My God, after they . . . nearly killed me? What the hell else do they want?

To finish the job? I'm not even going to testify against them. What did I ever do to them?"

"Nothing. You did nothing to them. You did nothing to deserve what happened to you. But now, with seven of their members dead and one more with a permanent limp, they are probably after two things."

Peyton clutched her purse; it was like a security blanket.

Brock continued, "They are likely seeking revenge for the deaths of their *brothers*." He let the word roll off his tongue like spoiled vinegar. "In some pathetically sick way, they are of the mindset that they should be able to do anything they want, and if something happens to them in the process, they consider it an offense."

Peyton's jaw dropped.

"I know, I know. Will and I have been in a lot of real shitholes in the world. We've been in bad places with bad people. And, we've seen this mentality before. Pure barbarians."

The hatred Peyton felt soaked out of her skin. "Those bastards." She felt a lump forming in her throat but quickly choked it back.

Brock stood, then knelt down beside her, placing one hand on her knee. "Let it turn," he said. There was salt in his voice. "Let it turn. Let the sadness and fear turn into anger."

"Oh, there's plenty of that inside me already."

"Good, because you're going to need it. Anger can get you through. Anger can clarify the mission, and anger can keep you warm at night."

Peyton cleared her throat, but a single tear made its way

down the smooth skin of her cheek. "You said they wanted two things. What's the second?"

"Most likely, it's as simple as them wanting you out of the way ahead of the felony trial that is about to take place. The one still in custody is on trial for rape and attempted murder. Even though you say you're not going to testify, to them, that's not good enough. In their way of thinking, they want to remove all doubt by taking you out of the picture. There would no longer be a star witness who could change her mind."

"But the cops have all the video surveillance tape. Even if I were dead, or couldn't testify, he'd still get convicted."

"Probably, sure," Will said. "But keep in mind we're not talking about rational-thinking adults here. We're talking about predators, and predators understand only one thing, violence."

"Yeah? Well, I'd like to make them understand violence, all right," Peyton replied.

Will glanced over his shoulder from his seat behind the steering wheel. "Now that's more like it. Kick ass. Hand them all up to the Almighty. Let him sort it out. That's what I always say."

Will and Brock laughed.

"I don't know how to thank you for what you are doing," she said.

Brock held up both hands. "There's no need. It's something that just had to be done. Someone needed to step in that night, and someone needs to step in now. It just happens to be me, that's all."

Will piped up, "Hey, what am I? Chopped liver?"

"Oh, sorry. Us, it had to be us. Almost forgot about grandpa over there."

Peyton giggled at the banter. "You guys have known each other a long time, haven't you?"

"I'll let the gray-haired historian over there talk about that."

Will said, "How much do you want her to know?"

"Tell her everything. She might as well know everything. She has to know who we are, otherwise, she'll never trust us." Brock looked down at his black leather boots, studying the laces. "Miss Phoenix, I'm going to warn you though. You might not like what you hear. I've done some pretty awful shit in my life." Then he looked her straight in the eye. "But I swear to you, I've never hurt a woman, and I never will."

"I believe you," Peyton whispered. "But, it's Peyton. You can call me Peyton."

Brock grinned. "Okay, *Peyton*."

A DARK PAST

When Will started to speak, Peyton wasn't quite sure what to expect. Perhaps the two had been outlaws or something, but it could be worse. Never in her wildest imagination did she anticipate the words that rolled out.

"Miss Phoenix," Will started.

"Peyton, it's okay, really, you can call me Peyton."

"Yes, ma'am. The first thing you should know about us is that Brock and I have worked together for years." Will cleared his throat in preparation. "You should know right off the bat, it's like he said, we've done some pretty awful shit together. We used to work for the government. They got to both of us when we were young and stupid. Being much older than Brock, I was there first, of course. And when pretty-boy there arrived at the Farm, he was greener than a blade of grass on a spring day. I was Brock's mentor."

"Mentor for what? What farm?"

"CIA, Miss Phoenix. We were CIA. The Farm is the CIA's nickname for Camp Peary in Williamsburg, Virginia, where we trained."

"Okay." Peyton wasn't sure where to go with the statement. "What did you do for the CIA?"

"Black ops." Will didn't avert his eyes from the narrow, two-lane road as the RV rumbled along. "We were covert operatives. We'd be called in for," he paused a moment, searching for the words, "for special situations."

"What kind of special situations?"

"The kind where the United States government perceives a threat," Will said.

"And what did you do when you got there?" Peyton asked.

"We were assassins, Miss Phoenix. We killed people for a living. We killed people for God and country."

The silence hung thick.

"It gets worse," Will continued. "We became disillusioned with the CIA after a while. We didn't believe in what we were doing anymore. So, we left. We went out on our own. We became contractors, hired to do the same type of work. We were hired by foreign governments. We no longer even had the justification of the US government behind our missions. We killed people for money, Miss Phoenix."

Peyton didn't know what to say but finally got her voice to return.

"And do you still kill people for money?"

"No, ma'am. We got out of that business a long time ago," Will said, "and haven't looked back."

"And what do you do for a living now?"

"Ma'am, we made so much money killing folks, we don't need to work anymore."

Brock said, "I ended up in Texas because I like the people and figured I could disappear into a small town. I chose Pearland because I wanted to be near the beach." He shrugged. "The old man here ended up in California. He likes the beach, too. But we kept in touch. He comes down here every once in a while to check up on me." Peyton could feel the bond between them.

Not a word was uttered for over five minutes as Peyton processed the information. The RV trundled across the narrow toll bridge and onto the Bluewater Highway, leaving a trail of salty sand in its wake.

Peyton rose from the bench seat and put one hand on Brock's shoulder and one on Will's. The men looked at her. "Teach me."

"Ma'am?" Will said.

"Teach me. Teach me what you know. Teach me how to defend myself. But, I want more than that. I want you to teach me how to kill them."

"Peyton," Brock said, "teaching you how to defend your-self is one thing, but teaching you how to kill people? I mean, you don't know what you're asking. Killing is . . . killing another human being can rip your soul. You don't want—"

"Stop right there," she said as she dug her nails into his broad shoulder. "My soul was ripped to pieces in that goddamn bar. Now, it's my turn. Killing them will stitch my soul back together."

23

MISTAKEN IDENTITY

Bailey Bank and Trust

The bank manager, Mr. Lawrence, walked up to Kiki. "Kiki? Listen, I know it's not your job, but Miss Phoenix has not returned from lunch, and that customer has been waiting at her desk. Would you mind going over there and helping him out?"

Kiki looked over her shoulder at Peyton's desk at the man waiting there. She turned back to Mr. Lawrence. "Of course," she said. And knowing what he wanted to hear, she added, "The customer is always first." She smiled politely and went to Peyton's desk. She extended a hand to greet the customer then sat down.

A few seconds later, with sudden ferocity, the double glass doors flung open and crashed into their door frames.

Four masked men charged in, each holding a sawed-off shot-gun. "Nobody move!" one screamed as he fired a round of buckshot into the ceiling. Bits of white plaster debris rained down.

Several customers screamed, and some went to the ground or ducked behind a piece of furniture. Two of the bank robbers jumped up onto the counter and ordered the tellers to empty their cash drawers. "And none of them explosive dye packs!" Another grabbed Mr. Lawrence and threw him to the ground.

The one who seemed to be in charge began barking orders. "You give us trouble, we'll cut you in half! You coop-erate, nobody gets hurt."

Three female tellers began emptying their cash drawers into bags, but a fourth had frozen. Her eyes were locked on the barrel of the shotgun. The robber standing above her yelled, "Move it, bitch!" But she remained motionless, as if in a trance. The man kicked her in the face with his steel-toed boot, and she fell to the ground. He leveled the shotgun at her and fired. The blast slammed into her abdomen causing her body to rock off the ground. She was dead within seconds.

"Goddamnit!" the one in charge yelled at the shooter. "Well, she ain't going to help you load that cash bag now, is she?"

The shooter hopped to the ground behind the teller counter and loaded the bag himself.

One of the others, a short, barrel-chested man, came out from behind the teller counter with a bag of cash in one hand

and his shotgun in the other. He walked up to Kiki and stared at her. The robber glanced down at the nameplate on the desk which read, "Peyton Phoenix." He looked back at Kiki. "What did you say to me?" he said to her.

Kiki shook her head, but no sounds came out.

"Keep your hands off that alarm button!" he yelled at her, though Kiki's hands were flat on the desk. "I said, keep your hands off that alarm!"

Kiki began to scream.

The man raised the sawed-off shotgun and discharged both barrels. Kiki's body flew backward, and the office chair flipped back. The man opened the shotgun's action by thumbing open the top lever. The barrels pivoted down on a hinge, exposing the breach. He pulled out the two spent hulls and dropped them to the ground, then reloaded.

Seconds later, the one in charge called out, "Let's get out of here!"

The four men ran back through the front doors, hopped into a car parked on the sidewalk, and tore off.

Mr. Lawrence removed his arms from covering his head. He then looked up and could see Kiki, who he had just sent over to Peyton's desk, laying motionless on the floor. He walked behind the counter and saw the teller covered in blood. She was dead as well. The smell of blood and gunpowder hung thick in the air.

24

KILLER BACKGROUND

At Surfside Beach, they ran out of road. Will turned the RV inland, drove northwest and then north over a series of back roads until they came to a "T" intersection and a lonely stretch of road called Hoskins Mound.

There Will turned northeast. The road was utterly straight. For four miles, there was nothing to see but scraggly oak trees silhouetted against the dimming sky.

In the darkening light, they turned left onto a short dirt driveway and pulled up to a dusky old clapboard cabin with windows trimmed in hurricane shutters.

Will pulled the RV around back.

"This is where Brock and I come to get away from it all." Will said. "Completely isolated. Completely off the grid. No internet. No one even knows the building is here, including the IRS," Will said as he laughed.

"Yeah," Brock said. "And defensible. One way in; one

way out. With the Brazoria Wildlife National Refuge at our back. It's a beautiful thing." It was the first time Peyton had seen him smile.

Once inside, Will flicked on a lamp and the wavy glow of orange-yellow light cast across the interior of the rustic cabin. Peyton could see the spartan dwelling had been hand-built right down to the rough-cut wood floors.

"Did you guys build this yourselves? My dad used to build. He would take me out to the job site when I was little. These walls are hand-lathed plaster, aren't they?" The men didn't answer.

After Will placed a heavy cardboard box on a table and switched another lamp on, Brock said, "Are those the dossiers?" The table was the only one in the cabin. It was a heavy, circular table, hand-hewn from oak with legs made from thick, straight oak branches.

"Yeah," Will replied. "I've been pouring over them."

"What dossiers?" Peyton interrupted.

"These are the files on each member of the Lincoln Killers gang." Will turned to Brock. "Those that are still alive, that is. All of these guys have rap sheets as long as my Johnson. Oh, sorry, ma'am."

"You don't have to call me ma'am," Peyton said.

Brock stepped up, "But it's this file that bothers me most."

"What is it?" Peyton said, stealing a glance into Brock's eyes.

Brock exhaled, then glanced at Will.

"Tell her," Will said.

"Peyton, this intel is the kind of data we would have gathered before we would go on an op. We'd make damn sure we knew what we were getting into first. This is intel on the overall Lincoln Killers gang, not just individual members."

"Compadre, Jesus man, spit it out," Will complained. "She's been through hell and survived it. She's tougher than you think."

"This gang isn't just some group of local street thugs. They're part of a national organization. The ones you ran into that night were just locals. The greater organization stretches into most everywhere in the country."

"Okay," Peyton said, "But how does that matter? It's these locals that attacked me."

Brock put both hands on her shoulders and looked deep into her eyes. For a moment, she thought she might melt. "Peyton, what we're saying is that even if all the locals were gone, that wouldn't be enough. These guys swear a blood oath. In fact, they have to kill a rival gang member or cop as part of their initiation. That's why the cops and feds can never get any undercovers inside their organization. It means this is never going to be over for you. They'll hunt you down. They'll spend all the time they need to make sure the job is done."

Peyton went weak in the knees, and Brock helped her onto the old leather couch. "I know, it's a lot to take in," he said.

Peyton was so entranced with Brock's steely looks that she almost allowed herself to be distracted from the threat of death. "My whole life," she said. "My whole life changed that night. Those goddamn bastards." She shuddered. "And it's never going to go back to the way it was, is it? I'm going to have to run, forever?"

"I'd lay down my life to keep you safe." Brock meant what he said. "I even knew I could be killed that night."

"Then why did you do it? Why did you risk everything to save me? You didn't even know me."

"Maybe some other time," was Brock's only answer. He was obviously uncomfortable revealing too much about his innermost thoughts. "That's why we're going to train you. If you are always going to be in danger, you need to be able to take care of yourself. We're not just going to teach you about weapons and hand-to-hand. We're going to teach you where to get a false identity, how to stay off the grid, how to change your appearance. It's the best we can do for you."

"Look at me," she said. "No, the two of you, just take a good look." Peyton stood and watched Brock's eyes run down her sleek form. "I weigh 118 pounds, wet. I don't know anything about self-defense, and you're going to train *me*?"

"When we're done with you, these shoulders and arms are going to be lean muscle. You're going to know how to shoot multiple weapons. You'll know how to break them down and repair them. You'll be an expert in demolitions, in setting up perimeter defense systems to alert you to any incoming threats. You'll know how to handle a knife, to survive in the wilderness for days, how to live off the grid."

"You're going to teach me to kill people, aren't you?"

"Not people," Brock continued, "animals, thugs. The first lesson starts right now, and that is that you have to learn to think of them as animals. They're not human and don't deserve your pity."

Peyton thought back to her one unknown, private variable—she still had no idea how far she would go if driven hard enough. *Can I kill someone?* The thought would not leave her. And then other thoughts coursed their way across her frontal cortex. *What about my old life? What about my apartment? What about my friends?* And then she remembered Kiki, her coworker, her best friend.

Brock's reassuring voice met her at just the right moment. "Peyton, I know what you're thinking. I can see it in your face. You're thinking about all the changes. I want you to embrace something; this is your new life. This is your new normal." It sounded like a sound-bite from a movie, but this was no movie, this was real, and it was happening right now. "I want you to get some sleep. It's late. In the morning, this won't all look so bleak. Remember, you're safe here. We're here to protect you."

Peyton hadn't realized it, but the stress of the day had taken a toll. She was exhausted. "Okay, where do I sleep?"

"Right over here," motioned Brock. "Why don't you take this bedroom. It's mine, but I'll sleep out here on the couch."

"Oh no. I can't put you out. You've done so much for me already."

"I won't hear of it. There's a bathroom in there as well. Get some sleep, and in the morning, we'll have breakfast and talk about our plans. We've got a lot of work ahead of us."

Will added, "Yeah, and I make a hell of a good cappuccino."

They were trying to cheer her up, and it was working.

25

INVESTIGATION

Bailey Bank and Trust

The man walked up to the police tape and held out a badge. "Special Agent Wilmont, FBI." He did not wait for the officer to grant him permission to enter the crime scene. Wilmont ducked the tape and walked through the open doors of the bank. He surveyed the carnage. One white female, about twenty-six years of age, lay on the floor with blood all over her blouse. Her eyes were open. The police photographer stood over her snapping photos, the bright flashes strobing in an all too familiar way.

The site did not shock Wilmont, but something did catch his eye. "Dammit!" he yelled. Other detectives and uniformed officers turned. "Haven't you people ever been briefed on what to do after a bank robbery?" Wilmont continued. "Why are all these people in my crime scene? Why haven't newspapers been laid across the countertops to preserve any fingerprints? How much evidence has already been destroyed?"

Outside, as Lt. Whelan arrived on the scene, the uniformed officer keeping people behind the police tape said to him, "Better watch out. A storm is brewing in there."

Whelan ducked under the crime scene tape and replied, "So what else is new?" He walked through the glass doors against the flow of out-coming officers. He grabbed the police photographer by the arm. "No, Charlie, you can stay."

Agent Wilmont spun around. "I thought I told you people to get out of here and quit destroying my evidence."

"Relax, Wilmont," Whelan replied. "No one's going to steal your crime scene. We know, bank robbery is FBI's jurisdiction." Whelan looked at the dead body of Kiki. "But it looks like this is more than a bank robbery."

"Yeah, yeah, yeah," Agent Wilmont said. "I know, murder is a *state* crime. You've told me that before. There's another one behind the counter, by the way."

Whelan ran his eyes across the debris scattered on the floor. "Looks like they really screwed the pooch on this one." He knelt down and put his face close to the back side of a shotgun shell. "Federal brand. Twelve-gauge, double-ought buck." Whelan stood and shook his head. "Not going to be easy to trace that. Those rounds are available in every gun shop, Walmart, and hardware store in the country."

"Tell me something I don't know," Wilmont said.

They surveyed the scene once again as the police photographer continued his work. They walked behind the counter and looked down at the other dead woman. "It's a damn shame," Wilmont said. "Look at them. Neither victim can be even close to thirty years old. Snuffed out. And for what? A little money?"

"Does this match the MO of any other bank robberies the Bureau is tracking?"

"Not in the five-state area, no," Wilmont said without hesitation. "This looks sloppy to me. Come on, let's take a look at the footage from the surveillance cameras."

They walked into the bank manager's office and found the recording device.

Whelan said, "That thing has got to be fifteen years old. What is that, tape?"

"Yup," Wilmont replied, "this thing was state-of-the-art back when I graduated from Quantico." He hit the rewind button, and the tape squealed into reverse. When it had finished rewinding, he clicked the play button, and they turned to the black and white monitor. As the scene unfolded, they both leaned closer to the screen. When it had finished playing, a scowl formed across Whelan's face. "So why kill the two women? I don't get it. Neither one of them appeared to be giving them any trouble."

"I've seen this kind of thing before in bank robberies. Sometimes the heat of the moment gets to them. Like I said, this job looks sloppy. But take a look at this guy here," he said as he pointed to one of the masked gunmen. "Throughout the whole thing, he's the calm one. Like he's done this before. But these others, look how jumpy they are. They look like kids, almost like this was their first time."

"So, the teller, she just looks frozen. Like maybe this guy is yelling instructions to her, but she's not moving."

"I guess he just got pissed off that she wouldn't respond. But it's not that one that bothers me. It's the other." Wilmont fast-forwarded the tape until the gunman approached Kiki. "See his mouth move? He's yelling something at her, and she is shaking her head in return. And then he just kills her. Something doesn't add up about this."

"Hey, Charlie," Whelan said to the photographer still busy at his work. "Did you hear the bank manager say anything?"

"Yeah," Charlie replied, "he said something like the shooter accused her of attempting to set off the silent alarm. Then he just shot her."

Wilmont rewound the tape, and they watched again. "Her hands are flat on the desk," Wilmont said. "In order to trip the alarm, she would have had to reach under the desk and press both buttons at the same time."

"Both buttons?" Whelan said.

"Yeah, it's a double-sided button device. You've got to apply pressure to both sides at the same time. That way, there's no chance you accidentally bump it with your knee and set it off."

Whelan leaned closer to the video monitor and squinted at the nameplate sitting on the desk where Kiki had been shot. "I can't read that; did you get her ID?" He and Wilmont walked out of the manager's office and over to the desk.

They looked at the nameplate. It had been knocked askew but otherwise sat upright.

"Peyton Phoenix," Wilmont said as he scribbled the name down in a notepad then looked at the dead girl. He glanced at Whelan whose face had turned a shade of white. "What's the matter?"

Whelan stared down at the body of Kiki. "That's not Peyton Phoenix." He placed a hand on his chin, and his eyes traced the ceiling as if lost in thought. "What if . . . what if this was a hit?"

"What you talking about?"

"Peyton Phoenix! This is where she worked. She was the victim in the Lincoln Killers gang assault case. The one you and I were talking about. What if this was a hit masked as a bank robbery? The bank robbers, they could be part of the Lincoln Killers gang, and they were here to take out Miss Phoenix before the trial."

Agent Wilmont looked at Kiki. "And you're sure that's not her?"

"Positive."

"Let's get out an APB on any member of the Lincoln Killers gang. We need to get their whereabouts and start bringing them in for questioning."

Whelan spun around and looked out the glass doors. "So where is Peyton Phoenix?" But then another thought occurred to him and he said, "The captain is sure going to be pissed about this one."

26

THE MORNING LIGHT

The Cabin

The next morning the sun shone through one of two windows in the bedroom. Peyton looked around from the comfortable bed. She thought back to last night when she had first climbed in. She could still smell Brock on the sheets, and it was nice.

As she'd drifted to sleep, the one thing she wished she had, however, was the warm feel of Brock laying next to her. This wasn't a sexual urge, it was just the yearning to have someone to hold; another softly beating heart to be next to.

The men had been right, however. Now, with light pouring in from the east, everything looked so much brighter, more positive somehow. The feeling of gloom inside the pit of her stomach faded, and Peyton could smell freshly-brewed coffee. It reminded her of being back home with her parents.

She got up and tiptoed to the closet. As she peered inside, she felt a little like she was prying, but not so much that she stopped herself. Brock's clothes were pressed and hung neatly on hangers, each with a uniformed amount of space between it and the next. There were shelves in which t-shirts, jeans, and other items were folded neatly. The stacks of clothes were so tight and in-line with one another, they looked like they had been folded by a robot.

Peyton ran her hands across the row of button-down dress shirts. *Should I?* she thought. Without wasting another moment, she dropped her shirt to the ground and slipped the white button-down over her shoulders, then buttoned it up. The shirt dwarfed her petite frame. Sleeves hung well past the length of her arms, and the shirt tails went down to mid-thigh.

She walked into the main room and found Brock pouring a cup of coffee.

"Good morning," she said.

While still pouring, Brock replied, "Morning." But when he turned and saw her, he became so distracted that the coffee overflowed the cup. "Oh, crap. Damn, that's hot. Ah, sorry." He couldn't avert his eyes, and Peyton grinned.

"Sorry, about the shirt, I mean. I hope you don't mind."

"No, not at all. You look, you look great in it." Payton wondered if he was imagining what she must look like with no shirt on at all. "Did you sleep all right?"

"Like a rock."

Will walked out from the second bedroom, "Well good, little lady. Because today, you're going to need your rest." He looked at her bare legs, slender and shapely, then said, "Man if I was twenty years younger."

Peyton blushed.

"Have a seat, I'll make you some breakfast," Brock said. "Today, we're going to start your training. Tonight, you will fall into bed exhausted, and not move until morning. We'll start out with a short run to get you warmed up, followed by some weight training and calisthenics. And right after that, firearms."

"Firearms?"

"You've got to know how to shoot."

* * *

After a run through the trails of the wildlife refuge, Peyton was already tired. She wasn't accustomed to exercise. And the push-ups and crunches were enough to bring her to her knees. But overall, she was exhilarated.

Will was a lot of fun as well. He was always in step, right behind the two of them. It was like having a father or uncle to watch over her.

Just after lunch, they walked behind the cabin and down a little woodland trail that led to a small clearing.

"This is our shooting range for small-arms," Brock said. "I want you to hold something." He removed a small, concealed pistol from his waistband. "This is a Glock 42. It's chambered in .380 ACP. It's a smaller round, and I want to start you shooting a pistol that won't kick you in the teeth. It's unloaded."

Brock showed her how the semiautomatic worked, how to hold it, how to unload it, how to aim, and most importantly, how to always ensure it was pointed in a safe direction. "I want you to envision that the gun is firing one round every second."

"Why?" Peyton asked.

"Because if it's firing one round a second, you'll always keep it pointed in a safe direction."

He loaded the gun and put it in her hands, then did something that made her shiver; he stood behind her and reached around, placing both hands on top of hers.

Several minutes later, a few dozen shell casings lay in a disarrayed pile on the leaf-covered ground. "That's perfect," he said. "Will, ever seen a beginner nail targets like that?"

"You sure you haven't shot before, little lady?"

"First time, honest. I kind of like it though." Peyton felt empowered with the gun in her hands. And even though she'd never held one before, she felt as if she'd been shooting her whole life.

"You've got a talent for it, that's for sure," Brock added.

As the day progressed, they moved up to a slightly larger 9 mm Glock, then a semi-automatic AR-15 rifle chambered in 5.56 NATO. The stock of the rifle fit into the pocket of her shoulder as though it was born there. Peyton had a steady way of holding whatever weapon, and she exhibited perfect form.

"This is excellent," Brock said. "All right, it's getting

close to chowtime. Peyton, I want you to carry the AR-15 and pistol with you at all times, from now on. Understood? "

She stared into his eyes and almost lost her concentration, but managed to answer. "Yes."

"And, any time I look at you before or after chow, I want to see you loading, and reloading each weapon, then field stripping them. I want you to be able to break down a weapon and put it back together as fast as possible. You'll even learn to do it blindfolded."

Under Brock's command, Peyton felt so safe, so guided. It was as though she could spend an eternity with him and not mind it one bit.

27

BLINDSIDED

As they got back to the cabin, Will disappeared into the RV intending to turn on the radio and pick up a news broadcast. Monitoring local news channels from town would help them keep an eye on any situations they should be aware of.

Being this far from civilization though made reception difficult, but after a few moments, Will tuned-in to an FM station out of Houston.

"This is KPFT, with news, weather, and traffic on the fives. We come to you live, with breaking news. We are positioned just down the block from Bailey Bank and Trust in downtown Alvin. This is as far as the police will let us set up. Apparently, Bailey Bank and Trust, a fixture in this town since 1909, has been the victim of a brazen daylight robbery. Police are confirming that two bank employees are dead, and the robbers escaped with approximately $32,000 in cash. Both local police and federal investigators are on the scene but are not commenting further at this time. Names of the victims are being withheld pending notification of their relatives. But one employee we were able to speak with said that the victims were a bank teller and a mortgage agent. As more information comes forward, KPFT will be the first to let you know. For now, reporting live . . ."

Will switched off the radio and rubbed his eyes. "Shit," he said. He stepped down from the RV and went into the cabin. There was nothing to do but share the bad news.

When he walked in, Peyton was at the kitchen sink washing some potatoes. And just like she promised, the assault rifle was in her possession, slung across her back. She did not intend to leave it unattended until told otherwise.

"Where have you been, old man?" she said with a smile. "You got a girlfriend in that RV or something?"

"Don't I wish," he said. But there was a deadness in his voice, and Brock turned to look at him.

"What's the matter?" Brock said.

"It's not good," Will replied.

"What isn't?" Peyton asked as she dried her hands with a towel.

When Will didn't say anything, Brock spoke up. "You have news? Worse than we thought?"

"What's worse than you thought?" Peyton asked.

Will nodded to Brock.

"Whatever it is, you might as well tell her," Brock said.

"Tell me what?" came Peyton's reply. "You're starting to freak me out."

Will looked her in the eyes. "It's not so much that it's worse than we thought, but it's sooner than we thought. It's your bank, Ms. Phoenix. Something has happened."

The hand towel dropped to Peyton's feet, and her face washed free of expression. "What?"

"A bank robbery," Will said. "And it's not good."

The tension became palpable, almost as if the air inside the cabin had thickened.

Peyton's voice cracked. "Someone was hurt?"

Will nodded. "Two people."

Peyton covered her mouth with her hand. "Are they . . . ?"

"I'm afraid so," Will said. "The news didn't give out any names. But . . . " His voice trailed off.

"But what?" Peyton said as a tear rolled down her cheek.

"They did say one was a bank teller . . ."

Peyton gasped.

". .And a mortgage agent."

The thought played forward in her mind. "Kiki!" Peyton said. "No, no, no. It can't be. It just can't be."

Brock went to her and Peyton buried her head in his chest.

"I'm so sorry," Brock said to her.

After a few moments, Peyton looked up and then pushed him away. "It's my fault. Isn't it? This is all my fault!"

"No," Brock replied. "Of course, it's not."

Tears streamed down her face. "Oh no? That bank has been there forever, and it's never been robbed. Not once! And now, all of a sudden, somebody goes in there and kills two people?"

"Peyton," Brock continued, "it's not your fault. It's the fault of whoever robbed the place."

"Lincoln Killers," Will said.

Brock turned on him. "You don't know that."

"I don't have to know that, compadre," Will said.

"If it's them," Peyton said, "they were coming after me, weren't they?"

Neither Brock nor Will replied.

"They were coming for me. I just know they were." She shook her head. "Kiki was one of my closest friends. The poor thing. She must've been scared to death." Fresh tears streamed forth.

Brock said in a soft voice, "If you had been there, you would be dead right now."

"Better me than Kiki!" she screamed, then stormed out of the cabin.

Will lowered his voice. "This thing is already getting out of hand."

"Tell me about it," Brock replied.

"We are heading into Indian country, a place we've been many times. But this time, I'm afraid it will be different."

Brock looked at him. "What do you mean?"

Will said, "Indian country, no matter where we were, was always filled with unknowns. It's just that the unknowns came from outside, never from one on our own team."

"What's that supposed to mean?"

"You know exactly what it means." Will pointed toward the cabin door. "Her feelings are going to get in the way, and we are not going to be able to control her."

"You let me worry about that," Brock barked, but he knew Will was right.

As if to confirm his assertion, they soon heard the steady, deliberate firing of the AR-15.

28

THE TRUTH

The Cabin

Early February

As dusk approached, a glowing redness oozed from behind the horizon in the distance. The winter air was crisp, yet that same chill, which would normally have made Peyton shiver, had no effect. It was a strange change in her, and Peyton wondered if she was toughening up. She was sore and tired but had learned so much in the past few weeks that her confidence soared.

Still, there was the problem of Brock. Peyton was uncontrollably attracted to him, but every time they started to get into a conversation where she thought he might be interested in her, he'd suddenly change the subject.

Once, about four days prior, Peyton was sure. The conversation had drifted into the personal, and Peyton asked what the longest relationship he'd ever had was. It was an innocent question, and something not uncommonly asked. But Brock seemed to drift away from it, lost somewhere in a sea of thoughts. Peyton wondered what his distance meant.

Brock walked ahead on the trail as the three hiked back to the cabin just before dusk. Peyton allowed herself to fall behind and slowed until Will caught up with her. Her rucksack and rifle were heavy, yet she made no complaint; her muscles could now keep up with their new demands.

"Will? Can I ask you a question?" she said.

"Anything, little lady." His South Texas drawl was cute and reminded her of her own father.

"Tell me about Brock."

"He's a scoundrel and a liar and a no-good and can't be trusted," Will joked. "What about him?"

"Well, it's probably no secret that I like him."

"Now why would I know that? Maybe it's that every time I look at you, you're staring at him?" The two laughed.

"No, seriously, Will. I just, I can't seem to get inside his head. It's like I can tell he wants to tell me something, but he stops. Every time, he stops."

Will stopped walking. "All right. I wouldn't normally tell anyone these things. But, I think with you, things are different." He looked up the trail as Brock disappeared over the small rise. "There's a reason he won't get too personal with you. He's got a wall built around himself. I don't know much about this emotional shit, but he's walled himself off. And I know why."

"Did something happen?"

Will gazed into the redness of the darkening sky. "Did something happen. Yeah, something happened. It's a strange thing though. It wasn't until you were in the picture that it all seemed to surface again. It was about ten years ago. He and I were still Company back then. We'd been assigned to do a job in North Korea. It was ugly. I don't want to get into the details of it. Anyway, we worked with one other person at that time. The three of us were a team. Her name was Lori, and she was our communications officer, which just means she did all the technical stuff, hacking, secure communications with Langley and such. Well, it didn't take long before Lori and Brock had fallen for each other." Will laughed. "It was kind of sickening, to tell you the truth."

"Oh, you don't mean that."

"No, I don't mean that. They were inseparable. But man, we had to keep it a secret. Operatives getting emotionally involved with one another is a big no-no. Anyway, he was in love with her. And when I say, 'in love,' I mean it."

"What happened?"

Will walked past Peyton and stopped with his back to her. He glared into the fading light. "He and I were coming back from a surveillance mission, you know, doing some recon on a target we were to take out. Apparently, the North Koreans got wind of our little operation. They found out about Brock, but not about me or Lori." He looked down at his boots and shifted some dirt from one side of the trail to the other. "They sent someone, they sent one of their own operatives to kill him. But, he ran into Lori instead. By the time we got back, it was too late. The thing was, they didn't just kill her, they did things to her, bad things."

Peyton covered her mouth with her hand.

Will continued. "Brock was broken. He was a broken man. I've never seen anything like it."

"Is that why he went berserk when those bikers were attacking me?"

"Damn straight it was."

"That look in his eyes," she said. "I can barely remember it, but there was this look in his eyes when he was tearing them apart. I can't describe it."

"His eyes looked dead, didn't they?" Will said. "It's called the thousand-yard-stare, a time when you kind of loose contact with the rest of us, and go into your own world. At any rate, when he saw you in that bar, he saw Lori. That's why he acts the way he does around you. When he sees you, he sees her. When he trains you, he's training her. He's always blamed himself for Lori's death. He's always blamed himself for not being there to save her, and it's still tearing him apart inside."

"What do I do?"

"I'm headed back tonight; going into Pearland to check on those Lincoln Killer assholes. Got to keep tabs on them, so we know where we stand. When I'm gone, he needs to know who *you* are. He needs to understand that you are not Lori. Maybe then he'll get it into his thick head."

As darkness fell around them, they hiked up the trail

toward the cabin. Peyton said, "Sky's beautiful, isn't it?"

"Red sky at night, sailors' delight. It's going to be a beautiful day tomorrow."

29
___

SEE ME

After a quiet supper, Will was out the door, headed into Pearland to check on the Lincoln Killers. The sound of the Harley firing to life still carried with it something of a thrill for Peyton. Her attraction to biker-types was not limited to the look of a leather vest over tattoo-covered muscles. She liked the sound of the bike. She liked to hear the engine's power. And she had liked the way it felt when she rode with her arms around Brock's body. The feel of him, along with the heavy thunder of the motor was exhilarating.

Brock had been quiet at supper, and Peyton knew she'd have to be the one to break the ice. With Will out of the cabin for a prolonged period, it might be her only chance to be alone with him.

"I can get those," Peyton said, just before Brock began to do the dishes.

"No, no. It's not a woman's job to do the dishes."

"Where does that come from?"

"What?" Brock replied as he started in on a large pot.

"You aren't like any man I've ever known. Most men look at me like I'm just another chick. You know, just something to keep around the house to clean up, and," her voice trailed off, "to have sex with."

Brock's teeth clenched. Even the muscles on his jaw had the capacity to bulge, and it only added to his chiseled look. "It's my upbringing."

"Your parents? Did they teach you to respect women like that?"

Brock stared at her a moment. "No." She could tell he was on the verge of sharing something. "My father. My father was abusive. He was an alcoholic. The way he treated my mother was awful. I couldn't stand him. Well, I swore that I'd never be like that."

Peyton walked to him and let her hand creep onto his broad shoulder. Brock visibly reacted to her touch. At first, he appeared startled, but then settled into it. "I'm sorry," she said. "That must have been terrible for you."

"He'd come home drunk and go after my mother. When I was little, there wasn't anything I could do about it. He'd come home and hurt her, you know, hurt her that way. I never understood why she stayed with him. I guess she had no way out."

Peyton slipped in behind him and put both hands around his waist. He was so warm, and her tenderness seemed to disarm him.

He continued. "When I got bigger, I learned to hate him

like nothing I've ever hated before or since. I'd wait up, late. And when he got home, I'd go downstairs and pick a fight with him. He'd come after me, instead of my mother. But, as bad as it was, his rage had a chance to escape, and my mom would be spared."

Peyton hugged him tighter. She knew it was now or never and decided to make one solid effort to tear down the mental wall he was still clutching—his heartbreak over the death of Lori -- someone he had loved deeply.

"Brock?"

He turned his head toward her as she continued hugging him from behind. "Yes?"

"Who am I?"

"What do you mean?"

"I mean, who am I? To you. Who am I?"

"I don't know what you're asking. You're Peyton Phoenix."

She reached up high, and with the gentleness of a feather on silk, she ran her hand over his face, closing his eyes. "Close your eyes and tell me who I am."

Brock did not reply. Instead, Peyton felt a tremble in his chest and a change in his breathing. He seemed to be struggling to fight back his emotions before they surfaced.

Peyton continued. "When you see me, you don't really see *me*. You don't see me for me, do you?" Her voice was tender, like beads of water running off an oak leaf in spring. But, there was no answer. "There's nothing you can do to bring her back, Brock."

Brock gasped, still choking back his feelings.

"I'm not her. I'll never be her, Brock. When you look at me, that's what you see, isn't it? You see her. Now turn around. Turn around and look me in the eye."

With some hesitation, he turned.

"Saving me won't bring her back. I'm not Lori, Brock." Peyton wasn't sure if her knowledge of Lori would anger him, or bring him to his knees, but she prayed for the latter —it was the only way to break the barrier.

Brock could no longer hold back his emotions. He was silent, but tears came, and he pulled her closer. The two stood in silence for a few minutes. "I know. I know," he said. "I'm sorry. I didn't mean to treat you that way. I didn't realize how much seeing you made me think of her, but it did."

"Then say it."

"You are not Lori, Peyton Phoenix. You are not her."

"Brock?" She nodded to the bedroom.

He looked through the bedroom door at the flickering yellow light coming off a candle. "Are you sure?"

"Brock, they stole something precious from me. But I'm not going to let them steal the rest of my life. I'm going to live my life. I'm not going to give them that power." Peyton looked around the room, steeped in thought. "I'm taking it back. That power is mine and mine alone." She grinned at him. "I'm sure."

30

INTO THE STORM

It was nearing noon the next day when Will pulled up on the Harley and parked behind the cabin. Neither Brock nor Peyton heard a thing. As Will came in the front door and walked toward his room, he wondered where his two companions were, and glanced through the open doorway into Brock's room. There on the bed lay Peyton and Brock still deep asleep.

"Good morning, you two!" he laughed.

Peyton stirred and saw Will looking at them. She quickly covered herself, saying, "Oh, shit."

"Oh, don't worry about it none, little lady. You don't have anything I haven't seen a hundred times before."

Peyton blushed but decided there was no point in being ashamed in front of Will.

Brock startled out of his slumber. "Hey, old man."

Will continued the playful ribbing. "And I suppose

you're going to tell me that the two of you accidentally lost all your clothes, and needed to keep warm by sharing a bed together? Just for sleeping purposes, of course?"

"Oh, leave her alone, Will."

"I can take care of myself," Peyton said. "Besides, I don't embarrass that easily."

"Really?" Will said.

"Well," Peyton continued, "you two have told me so much about yourselves, things that you wouldn't normally tell anyone. I might as well do the same. If the truth be told, this isn't the first time I've been naked with a guy and seen by others before." She giggled.

"Really?" Brock said.

"Do you think less of me because of that?"

"Hell, no," Brock said.

The three laughed. It was apparent that their friendship was solidifying.

"Well, get the hell up," Will said. "We've got a lot to talk about. Besides, I'm starving."

"Yeah," Brock said, "time for breakfast."

"Breakfast, my ass. It's lunchtime, Romeo. Now get some clothes on that little Philly and let's eat. Oh, and put some clothes on yourself too. I don't want to see you all naked and stuff walking around my cabin."

"*Your* cabin?" Brock kidded. "I built it."

"Did not."

"Did too."

Peyton interrupted. "Honestly, you two are like a couple of kids."

"Nanner-nanner-boo-boo," Will teased.

* * *

After lunch, the three went on the back patio enjoying a respite from the chill, winter rains that had soaked the area overnight. Peyton drew in the aroma of fresh pine boughs.

Brock started. "So, what did you find out about our friends?"

Will's demeanor shifted. He was all business. "Anarchists. The Lincoln Killers think of themselves as anarchists. Buck the system, be beholden to no one, answer to no one, particularly not to the government, do whatever they please. You know the type."

"Yeah, I know the type," Brock said.

"Anyway, it's worse than we thought."

"What's worse?" Peyton asked.

"From the intel I could gather, it appears there were close to forty members of the local chapter. Now that Captain America over there took out seven of them, and incapacitated another, they're down to around thirty."

"So why is that bad?" Peyton said.

"Like I said," Will continued, "they're part of a national organization. I guess the boys that lead this group of miscreants don't take it lightly when some of their members wind up dead. Not to mention the upcoming trial of the survivor. The national gang leaders hired a thug attorney to defend him in court. And," Will looked at Peyton, "the cops are all over the place, looking for you. They're freaking out that you've disappeared. They want to know if you're alive for one thing. But they also want you to testify."

"Not likely," Peyton said. "I mean, it would be suicide. I'd probably never make it to the courthouse before being gunned down or run over by ten Harleys, or worse."

Brock said, "I'm glad you're on the same page with us about that. It's just too dangerous."

"But, there's also no way I'm going to just sit here either."

"We trained you to be able to defend yourself, not to go on a vigilante mission," Will quipped. "We trained you to kill, sure, but we have no intention of allowing you to go out and confront a bunch of hardened criminals. We're going to lay low, then we're going to get the hell out of here. Let us handle it."

"You may have trained me to defend myself, and only to kill as a last resort, but that was never my intent."

Brock leaned up and put his hand on her arm, "What do you mean?"

"I mean I've got enough pent-up rage in me to light up Hiroshima. I've thought of nothing else since the day I woke up from the attack. I'm going to kill those sons of bitches."

"I told you," Will said, glaring at Brock. "I told you this would happen. Now we've gone off and created ourselves a monster."

Brock knew he was right. "Shut up."

"I told you right from the start," Will jibed. "So, you may as well get on board with it. I knew it from the moment I met her. She's tougher than you think, and she's got a mind of her own. And now look at her. Look in those eyes. Shit, you can see the rage. Might as well get it over with. I say, cut her loose. She'll tear those assholes apart."

Brock let out a long exhale.

"Kill them?" he said to Peyton. "You want to go kill them? Tell me this, based on your training, how is it that you suggest that be done?"

"Well, we're highly outnumbered, right?" she replied. "Not to mention cops all over the place. It's like you said, when outnumbered, pick off the ones on the outskirts. I'll lure them one at a time, away from the others."

"How?" Brock said.

Will grinned as he watched the two of them.

"After all the reconstructive surgery done on my face, I don't look like myself from before the attack, right?"

"Right," he said.

"They won't recognize me. I'll lure one out of the main group. I'll seduce him. And when he's at his most vulnerable, I'll rip his guts out."

"She's scary," Will said, "but I like her. My kind of gal."

Brock didn't realize how much his feelings for Peyton were getting in the way and became incredulous. "You're going to lure one of those bikers by making him think you want to screw him, then you're going to kill him? Yourself? Are you insane?"

Peyton gazed out the window. "Stenolemus bituberus."

"What?" said both Brock and Will at the same time.

"*Stenolemus bituberus.* Also known as the assassin bug."

"Assassin bug? You're making that up, right? What are you talking about?" Brock asked.

She continued staring out the window, off into the horizon, as if in a trance. "Entomology was my favorite class in undergrad. The assassin bug is found across much of Australia. It hunts much the way I intend to."

Will leaned closer to Brock and whispered, "Hunts? Jesus, she's talking about *hunting* them now."

"It has two ways to hunt its prey." Peyton sounded distant. "It stalks its prey, sneaking up behind it, then attacks at just the right moment." A small grin peeled across her delicate facial features. "And, it also favors sneaking up to a spider web and flicking one of the strands of the web. The spider feels the vibration and thinks it's caught something, so it comes out to investigate. That's when the assassin stabs it with a sharpened part of its body." As the two men watched, Peyton pulled out the Glock 42 and slowly screwed the suppressor onto the end of the barrel. "I have a sharpened part of my body. It's right here. The others will never hear a thing."

"You're serious, aren't you?" Brock questioned. "You're serious as a heart attack. Peyton, this is really dangerous. Will and I planned on taking out the locals one at a time, but now that the national organization has sent in reinforcements, going after any of them is suicide."

"But, compadre," Will said, "let's think about this thing. You and I were talking about a frontal assault on the locals, right? You know, set up several packs of C4 explosives, create some kind of diversion in the middle of the night, send them all scattering out the front door, blow them to smithereens?"

"Wait," Peyton said, "You guys have been planning all this, and didn't tell me? You've been talking about hiding out this whole time, not a frontal assault."

But they ignored her. "What she's talking about makes a lot of sense. There's too many of them to take out at once. And think of it. Think of the fear we'll instill in these assholes. They'll see one dead body after the next after the next."

Brock stood tall and approached Will with his shoulders back. "You're buying into this shit?" Brock said as he pointed. "There's no chance I'm sending her into harm's way like that. You and I risking our asses in a firefight is one thing, but her? No way."

Peyton interrupted. "It isn't your choice."

Will finished the thought, "Well, there you have it. The little lady has made up her mind. Come on, compadre. You've got to admit, she's pretty damn nice to look at. She's tempting. I mean, look at her. Wouldn't you fall for it if a girl like that lured you toward her bed?" Will's expression suddenly lightened, "Oh wait, I'm sorry. That's not what happened to you last night, right? No, it couldn't be. Compadre, what was that thing you said? You said you both suddenly lost all your clothing and decided to get in the bed together, just to keep warm, right?" The sarcasm hung thick.

Brock could do nothing but grin and shake his head at Will. "You were always an asshole."

31

ANGER UNRESTRAINED

The national contingent of Lincoln Killers, led by president John Michael Brewer, aka, *Grinder*, finally roared into Pearland with Grinder at the helm. They wove through back roads until arriving at the ramshackle house used by local members as their primary hangout. It sat off Dixie Farm Road on the outskirts of town to the northeast of the bar. In Grinder's opinion, that was a good thing. A little distance between the main town and what was certain to be viewed as an eyesore kept local law enforcement at arm's length. He'd seen the mistake other chapters had made by choosing the wrong location, and he was glad to see that this chapter had, at least, done one thing right.

Grinder pushed the kickstand down and stepped off his Harley. His entourage followed suit and soon, bikes of all types were strewn across the torn-up lawn. He pulled off his thick black glasses and propped them on top of his head, then turned and surveyed the area. The four-lane, median-divided road was only sparsely traveled, though a 1950s-era shopping strip was located across from them.

He walked toward the front door, kicking a beer can out of his path on the way in. His second in command, Gears Pliskin, followed. The inside of the gang house was similar to many others he had visited. There were holes in the drywall, beer cans and other trash littering the floor, and gang members unconscious on couches or the floor. At this time of afternoon, most gang members were starting to stir, having slept away most of the day.

He walked toward the back of the house where he could hear a television. Grinder walked into the back room. The room was occupied by one man. He was seated in what had once been a leather-upholstered La-Z-Boy. It was now covered in duct tape to hold the stuffing inside.

The man appeared to be about thirty years of age, had black hair, and a thick, unkempt beard. A can of Budweiser was in his hand. The man looked at Grinder. "Who the hell are you?"

"The name is Grinder." He was expecting a response.

Suddenly realizing he was talking to the president of the national organization, the man stood. But instead of reacting with respect, he said, "So?"

Gears stepped out from behind Grinder. "I don't think I like your attitude," he said.

But Grinder put a hand on him. "This is how you greet the president?" Grinder said as he glared at the man.

The man replied, "We don't need any California pussies

coming down here from our national office to tell us what to do."

"You wouldn't need a visit from me if you ladies weren't so inept," Grinder said as he reared back and punched the man across the jaw. The man flipped over the La-Z-Boy, and beer flew against the wall. Grinder again held a hand up to prevent Gears or anyone else from stepping forward. He walked to the man, who was still on the ground, and grabbed him by the shirt, then yanked him to his feet. "You see, what I'd like to know is, how did you bunch of faggots lose seven members, and have an eighth beaten half to death, by just one man?" He reared back and drove a fist deep into the man's stomach.

The man doubled over and grabbed at his midsection. He slumped to the ground then looked up at Grinder and said, "Fuck you, man! I wasn't even there."

Grinder yanked him off the ground again and held him by the lapels. "You let one man kill seven of our patches? And what have you done to find him? Why isn't his head on a stake in here?"

The man replied, "We don't even know who he is. Never seen him before. Hell, man, nobody can find him. Not even the cops."

Grinder yanked the man closer. "When I was chapter leader, nobody got in our way. If they did, they were dead."

The man wiped blood from his mouth and pushed away from Grinder. "We don't need no national help. We can take care of our own."

"Oh yeah?" Grinder said. He grabbed the man and headbutted him in the nose. "And what about the bitch? She's still alive, isn't she?" The man flung backward and crashed onto the floor. "To me, it doesn't look like you can tie your own boots. And boots don't even have laces." He let the man lay there and turned to Gears. "Find out who the rest of these assholes are. See if any of them are worth a shit." As Gears turned away, Grinder added, "And find out what happened with the boys you sent down on that bank job."

32

THEY MISSED

Chopper Town Biker Bar, Pearland

The news of the debacle at the bank came later that evening. Grinder, holding court at the biker bar, was not happy.

"What do you mean they didn't get her?" Grinder yelled as he picked up a steel chair and flung it across the room.

"Sorry, boss," Gears said, "they missed."

"Missed? How could they miss? They were carrying sawed-off shotguns! They walked into a bank with one job—kill the girl and make it look like a robbery."

Gears looked down but tried to keep a confident tone in his voice. Weakness was not tolerated. "I talked to our bank job expert. He said those two new guys were worthless. Both of them panicked. One of them had the foresight to look at the nameplate on the desk before he blew away who he thought was our girl at least."

"You mean to tell me those dumbasses killed somebody, and it wasn't even the bitch we were looking for?"

"Its worse than that, boss," Gears said. "They killed *two* females."

"Two?" Grinder walked up and put his face next to Gear's, then crossed his arms. "They were sent in there to kill a skinny little white chick, and they killed two females, but neither was the right one? Those fucking idiots. Let me guess, we've got ten times as much heat coming down on this now. Am I right?"

Gears struggled to maintain eye contact. "Feds are all over this one. Must be a dozen new agents in town, just for this."

Grinder began to pace the floor as he collected his thoughts.

Gears said, "I've already had it taken care of, by the way. Both of those newbie hang-arounds who screwed up are dead. And I sent the other two guys who were involved in the bank robbery out. They'll be back in California by morning. Didn't want them anywhere around here, not after how bad they fucked this up."

"That saves me having to tell you to do it. Right now," Grinder said, "we're screwed, but at least you've closed some loose ends. There's going to be heat coming down everywhere on this one. And if they figure out we were targeting the Phoenix woman, the game is up. We'll never find her out in the open after this."

"On the bright side, boss, I sure as shit don't think she's going to testify."

Grinder rubbed his stubble–covered chin. "I don't like this. I don't like this one bit. You never know with a witness. She's a liability, and I don't like liabilities."

33

REVELATION

After hours of planning, and multiple efforts by Brock to talk Peyton out of her idea, Peyton's mind was made up. She knew exactly what she was going to do.

"I don't want you to do this," Brock said as he and Peyton stood on the back porch. "I'm scared. I don't want anything bad to happen to you."

"You act tough, Mr. Brock Paladin, but you have a soft side. You like me, don't you?" She was teasing him.

Brock replied, "No, be serious. I do like you. I more than like you. God, I never know what to say."

"Men are so bad at this," Peyton said as she laughed.

"Peyton, what I'm trying to say is that I care about you. I've cared about you for a long time. I think it started when I visited you in the hospital. And the more I've gotten to know you, the more worried I'm becoming about you heading into harm's way."

"I want to tell you something, something important," Peyton said. "Ever since that night, I've held this vision of you in my head. My memory is blurry, but I have these little flashes of your face. I've held onto those visions. I held onto them with all I've got. And then, I started seeing your face in the hospital. I was so drugged up at the time, it's hard to remember. It's not so much a memory of seeing you, it's a feeling I get inside whenever you're around me. It's like I can feel your presence. I've never felt like this about anybody. Brock, I think I'm falling for you."

Peyton's last statement hung in the air for a moment, and she was afraid she had said too much, almost afraid to breathe.

"I'm falling for you too. I know part of what happened was that I associated you with Lori, but that's all behind me now. I have feelings for you. I'm scared. I'm really scared. And not for my own life, for yours. I don't want to lose you."

Peyton went to him, and they kissed.

"Ahem," Will said as he stepped out onto the porch. "I'd tell you two to get a room, but you already have one. So, we're decided then? It's tomorrow?"

"Damn right," Peyton replied.

The three friends placed their hands on top of one another. The bond between them was strengthening.

34

THE TARGET

In the early morning before dawn, the three headed out in the RV and caught Texas State Highway 332 north to Lake Jackson and to the H-E-B Grocery store to get supplies – and an Internet connection.

Once parked, Will spun the driver's chair around, stood, and walked to a set of kitchenette cabinets, then opened one of the doors.

"Wait," Peyton said as she looked at what the cabinets contained: a bank of several video monitors. "These are views from surveillance cameras *inside* of their place? How did you get inside their hangout and install hidden cameras without being seen?"

Will laughed, "Done it a thousand times, little lady. I went in yesterday morning. These guys party into the night, but in the morning hours, they're out like a light. Besides, it's like we taught you; sometimes it's better to not sneak in and try to go undetected. There's too many variables."

"Right," Brock added, "you hide in plain sight. I don't even have to ask Will how he got these cameras in place. I can tell you, he went native. Look at the guy. He looks like he's a damn biker anyway. He just had to up the outfit a bit."

"That's right." Will paused a moment. "Hey, wait a minute. Was that a cut? You think you're so funny, compadre." He turned to Peyton. "Anyway, I put on another layer of leather, a dew-rag over my head, and some dark shades. Hell, a couple of them woke up when I was walking through their piece-of-shit house. They didn't bat an eye. They just figured I was one of their own."

"Not to mention," Brock continued, "that there are a bunch of gang members from the national organization, that are now staying at that place."

"And, it's not like these guys have a high school year-book to look at to make sure they know who's a member."

"No high school yearbook, huh?" Peyton laughed.

"No," Will said, "but I did find this." He pulled a catalog out from his waistband.

"A Sharper Image catalog? You're kidding me," Peyton said. "What, you think they're looking to spruce up the place?"

"Guess so," Brock said.

Will changed the subject. "Let's do a radio check."

Peyton adjusted the tiny transmitter in her left ear, and Will spoke into a microphone. "Miss Phoenix, can you hear me?"

"Yes," Peyton whispered back. "And you don't have to call me Miss Phoenix."

Peyton looked at Brock and noticed his brow had furled. "Peyton, are you sure about this?" he said. "It's not too late to back out. You don't have to do this."

"Bullshit," she replied. "If there's anything in my life that I *have* to do, it's this. I need this, Brock. I need this for me. I'll never be whole again otherwise."

Brock's face stiffened. "That's just a bill of goods you've sold yourself."

Instead of letting an uncomfortable silence ensue, Will said, "Weapons check."

Peyton pulled out the small Glock and checked the chamber to ensure a round was in place. She then affixed the silencer. She tucked it in the small of her back. She then pulled back her leather jacket to reveal a second Glock. Will pulled that gun out and checked the chamber.

"Killing can't make you whole again." It was the last thing Brock said to her before they headed out. Peyton sat up front. Her breathing was a little shallow, but she knew the Lincoln Killers gang had no idea that a firestorm was coming. The thought made her smile.

Brock and Will watched and exchanged nervous glances.

"It's go-time, compadre," Will said.

In minutes, they were rolling north on State Highway 288 toward Pearland.

35

FIRST BLOOD

Dixie Farm Road, Pearland, Texas.

After Peyton had stepped out and started walking across the street, Brock and Will were glued to the computer monitors in the RV. On the screens were the views from the hidden surveillance cameras. The RV was parked a hundred yards from the run-down dwelling, the overgrown lawn of which was strewn with Harley Davidson motorcycles and empty beer cans.

"She's really going to do this, isn't she?" Brock said as he rubbed his eyes.

"Damn straight. She's in deep kimchi now, compadre. Enemy territory for sure."

"I can't stand this. I've got to stop her."

But before Brock could stand, Will placed a vice-like grip

on his forearm. To Brock, Will's fingers felt like the talons of an eagle.

"You aren't stopping shit. You heard her, man. You saw the look in her eye."

"I'm falling for her, all right? I can't help it. I'm falling for her, and I'm scared. After she experiences the enormity of what killing another human being does to your insides, I'm afraid she won't be the girl I know right now."

"I hear you," Will said. "But, I don't think she's going to be affected by it the way we were."

"Why the hell not?" Brock said as he stood. "Killing is killing. It eats you from the inside out."

"You and I, we assassinated people for our country, and for money. Neither one of us ever had the type of motivation she has. You following me, compadre? This is something she *has* to do, and do alone. Otherwise, she'll always regret letting the animals live."

Both men caught motion out of the periphery of their vision and glanced at the monitors. "Shit, there she is."

Peyton was inside the hangout now. They watched as she moved from the front door slowly down the hallway, glancing in different rooms along the way. There were bikers sacked out in all corners of the trash-filled house. But Peyton walked in a natural, almost relaxed manner. To them, she may as well have been a woman out for a morning stroll on the beach. Yet, if a biker woke up from a drunken or drug-induced stupor, they would never suspect any wrongdoing was about to occur.

"What the hell is she doing?" Brock said. "Taking inventory? She's walking through the whole house. Jesus, pick one of them and get it over with already." He leaned into the microphone and said, "Peyton, what are you doing? You've got to get in and get out quickly like we talked about."

But Peyton was apparently not taking orders from anyone other than herself.

They watched as she removed the tiny speaker from her ear and placed it in the pocket of her black leather jacket.

"Oh hell, she's going off-script. We really have created a monster."

"Not a monster, compadre, a perfect weapon. Look at her. Were you that clear-thinking and level-headed on your first op?"

"Yes."

"Bullshit," Will quipped. "I was watching, remember? You looked like you'd soil your drawers at any moment. But this girl, damn, I've never seen anything like it."

"She hasn't killed anyone yet, if you hadn't noticed. What does she think she's going to do? Wake up one of them and tell him, hey, let's go outside and screw? This is so fucked up."

But as Peyton walked into the main room where five bikers lay strewn about, they watched as she slowly withdrew the smaller Glock from her jacket.

"Oh, God," Brock said. "She's not going to draw one of them outside, she's going to cap one of them right here and now. She's actually going to do it."

In quick succession, Peyton fired five silenced rounds,

each striking a sleeping biker square in the forehead. It happened so quickly the two men went speechless.

At last, Will stuttered, "Did we just see what I think we saw?"

"Holy shit, she killed five guys. She, she, she . . ."

But what they saw next shocked them even more. Peyton looked into one of the tiny, hidden cameras in a corner of the room. She was grinning, actually grinning. She walked to each freshly killed biker's body, kicked it over with her foot, and then fired another round into the groin area. It was her revenge. She was leaving a message—*you attacked the wrong woman.*

"She just shot those guys in the balls! Oh, shit," Brock said, almost screaming. "When the rest of them see that, they're going to know; they're going to know."

Peyton then withdrew something small from her back pocket and dropped it on top of one of the dead men.

"What did she drop on that dude's chest?" Will asked. "Her damn business card?"

They leaned closer to the monitors and watched as Peyton casually dropped an empty magazine out of the Glock and replaced it with a fresh one.

"Oh. man, she wouldn't," Brock said as he shook his head.

"Oh, yes, she would. Did you see how many clips she had on her waistband when she pulled her jacket back? And that's not all that was clipped to her hip!"

But before Brock could speak, Peyton walked into the

first room on the left. She aimed and fired three rounds in quick succession, exploding the skulls of another three sleeping bikers. Then, she stood over the top of each and fired a round into their groins.

"Another three!" Brock said. "Wait, what else is clipped onto her waistband?"

This time, the firing of her silenced Glock did not go unnoticed. Bikers from two other rooms stirred. Some words were exchanged, and they got to their feet. Before Brock and Will had even registered the threat on the video monitors, Peyton leaned into the hallway and began firing one silenced round after another as bikers swarmed out.

Several were hit, and chaos broke out.

It was then that Brock's question about what else was clipped to Peyton's belt was answered. He watched as Peyton yanked a canister-shaped device from under her jacket. He recognized it immediately. It was a white phosphorous hand grenade.

Peyton flung it diagonally into a room where several more members of the biker gang had jumped up. The resulting explosion rocked the view from the video cameras.

"Shit!" Brock yelled. "She's got Willie Petes! Those things explode at two thousand degrees. She'll burn the house down!"

Peyton removed the larger Glock, tossed a second white phosphorous grenade into the back room, and simultaneously fired the Glock into the confined space. The gang members inside never stood a chance.

The entire event took less than a minute. The feed from the video cameras was cut except for one which showed a view from the front door and down the main hallway.

Brock and Will watched as Peyton moved into each of the two rooms where grenades had been thrown. Smoke was starting to billow from each. They could not see what was happening in those rooms, but they assumed she was leaving her macabre calling card: a round in the groin of each dead biker.

"Come on, we've got to get her the hell out of there," Brock said.

"She's already on her way out."

Peyton walked underneath the remaining operational video camera and smiled into it. The entire scene looked like the result of a SEAL team raid on an Al-Qaeda safehouse.

"Start the RV," Brock called. "I'm going to meet her on the street." He was out the door. He rounded the back corner of the shopping center and saw Peyton strolling across the street with all the air of a person walking the dog. He stopped and watched. It was unlike anything he'd ever witnessed. This girl was acting like a hardened assassin. She continued her casual walk until she reached Brock. She took little notice of the shock plastered across his face, and simply picked up his hand and pulled him toward the approaching RV.

Will pulled up next to them and leaned out the window.

"We might want to get the hell out of here before the fire trucks and cops get here."

As they drove out of the parking lot, they looked across the street. Smoke billowed from it, and a window blew out as flames erupted inside the structure.

36

THE CONFRONTATION

Brock collapsed into one of the seats at the rear of the RV. Peyton stood by Will who was steering them out of the area. "Any trouble?" she said.

He only looked at her.

"Will, anyone following us?"

"Not that you would have noticed. Good god, little lady. You go from damsel in distress to cold assassin. Shit, it's like watching Linda Hamilton in that *Terminator* movie. Where the hell do you get off killing all of them? You have any idea what kind of heat that's going to bring?" He turned back, but she had already retreated to go sit by Brock. "Damnedest thing I've ever seen."

* * *

Two hours later, the RV was once again hidden behind the remote cabin. Will left the two in the RV and went inside. "There's going to be so many Lincoln Killers swarming around that town . . . there won't be enough bullets." He turned on the radio to listen to the KPFT news broadcast.

". . . reporting live. We're outside a home that, up until about an hour ago, was fully engulfed in flames. Police and fire investigators are on the scene now, but early reports indicate there may be a significant number of victims. Here's police Lt. Dan Whelan. Lieutenant Whelan, what can you tell us?"

"It appears that a large number of individuals have been found inside the structure. All are deceased at this time."

"You say 'a large number.' Can you be more specific?"

"We have an initial body count of thirty individuals."

"Did you say thirty? Should we assume from the police presence that foul play is suspected?"

"I can't comment on an ongoing investigation," Whelan said. He walked back toward the charred remains of the home.

"You heard it here first," the news reporter said. "We'll bring you more information as we get it. Apparently, thirty individuals are dead, victims of this extensive house fire. Reporting live from the scene, KPFT News Radio 90.1."

Will turned off the broadcast. *"Thirty.* Good God. The

national organization is going to flood this state with low-life thugs."

Brock stood in the open doorway with a look of resignation on his face. "Will, she did what she did, okay? It's over. What's done is done."

The two men stood face to face.

"Blowback," Will said.

"Blowback?" Peyton replied from behind Brock. "What is that supposed to mean? They got what was coming to them."

"They got what was coming to them? Did all of them attack you that night?" Will pressed. "Hell no. They got what was coming to them, my ass." He paced the room. "Blowback. It's the result of the unintended consequences of a mission. You carry out a mission, but didn't foresee the repercussions, or, didn't take the time to think them out in advance."

"Will, look, I was a little pissed off too," Brock said. "But the more I've thought about it, the more I understand what Peyton did. She did what she had to do. Hell, this is our fault. We trained her."

"You don't have to defend me," Peyton said. "And Will, I'll come straight to the point. I don't care if not all of those thirty attacked me. In my mind, they're all the same. They're a bunch of lawless women-haters, and I say kill them all. They got exactly what they had coming to them."

"I'm not saying they're not a bunch of low-life's that deserve to be on the smoking end of a gun barrel, but dammit! Now we'll have the whole Lincoln Killers organization flooding this area," Will groused. "They're going to be looking for revenge. And you've drawn Brock and me into the middle of it. You used us. You fucking used us. You knew we could train you to defend yourself, and you took it upon yourself to go on a full-scale vigilante mission! We're dead, you know that? We're all dead." He turned and pointed a sharp finger at Brock. "And you, Romeo. You're on her side. She just signed your death warrant, and yet you're going along with it. And why? I'll tell you why. Because—"

"Don't you say it," Brock warned.

"Because you're screwing her!"

Brock pounced like a cat on a mouse and struck Will across the jaw, knocking him to the ground. Peyton jumped in front of Brock. "No, Brock, stop! It's not his fault!"

She knelt down to Will, but he pushed her away. He wiped blood from his mouth and then stood. "You get that one for free, compadre. But after all we've been through, you're going to let a woman come between us?"

"That's not what I want!" Peyton pleaded.

"Blowback, Missy," Will said. "Unintended consequences. You've put us into the center of the crosshairs."

Brock studied the tops of his boots. "Will, I'm sorry. I shouldn't have hit you. I lost my temper when you said that. It's just . . . it's just that I've fallen for her."

Silence hung in the room.

"You've fallen for me?" Peyton said.

Will shook his head. "I knew it. Son of a bitch. Fallen for another pretty face." He moved until he was face to face with Brock. "You look me in the eye and tell me the truth."

Without hesitation, Brock said, "I think I love her, man."

Peyton clenched her hands to her mouth.

"All right, dammit, all right," Will said as he let out a long exhale. "Well, we're in deep kimchi now. But, we're in it together."

37

THE MORNING SEDUCTION

The Cabin

Later that night, the three talked about their plans. From all indications, there would likely be no evidence left at the scene that could be traced back to them. The fire consumed the entire structure and would have easily melted the shell casings ejected from Peyton's weapons. Even the bullets that were embedded in the charred corpses would likely be mangled beyond identification. There had been no one on the street and no security cameras outside the shopping center with a view of the scene. They agreed to immediately destroy the footage that they had been recorded from their own surveillance cameras inside the biker hangout.

"I wonder what they do with all those bikes," Peyton said. Her face was devoid of expression.

"What bikes?" Brock asked.

"All those Harley's. Thirty dead bikers, thirty owner-less Harley's. That entire house is gone, but those bikes were all sitting in the front yard."

Brock laughed. "I don't know, I never thought about it."

Will leaned up from his reclining position on the couch. "Is that what you're thinking about, Miss Phoenix? You pop thirty bikers, shoot most of them in the nuts, and you want to know what the cops are going to do with their choppers?"

"If you're wondering if I'm all remorseful, the answer is no. I feel nothing." Her eyes glazed over. "When I was in there, it was like I was watching myself from above. Like I was watching a movie. I felt nothing. Now that it's over? When I look back on it, it just feels . . . it feels, I don't know, exhilarating. It feels like a new start."

* * *

When morning light again flooded the bedroom, Brock awoke to find Peyton staring at him.

"Well, good morning to you too," he said. "You all right?"

"I could stare at you all night."

"Don't you ever sleep?"

"No," she laughed.

"But are you okay? I mean, is it sinking in?"

"Brock, I don't know how to explain it. Something snapped in me the night I got attacked. It just snapped. I knew I'd never be the same. I knew it would change me, but I didn't know how far it would go."

"What do you mean?"

"After the attack, I wanted everything to be fine. I wanted to just go back to being me. But I couldn't. It's like, I wasn't me anymore. That knowledge scared me. I didn't know if I liked who I'd become. But then I found you. You channeled me. Channeled me in a direction I didn't know I could go. There was so much anger in me. It was eating me alive. And once you trained me, I knew my anger had a place to go."

"You knew exactly what you were going to do, didn't you?"

"I've never known how far I'll go in any given situation. But, I think I knew it from the first time you showed me how to shoot. I knew it right then. Holding that gun in my hand . . . it felt like power. I became drunk with it, and I still am drunk with it. Brock, even if you two hadn't stuck with me, I would have walked in that biker hangout and killed as many as I could, no matter what the consequences. I wanted revenge."

"But that's not all, is it?"

"Now that I've gotten revenge, I want more."

"I know you must have had an unbelievable amount of anger at them, but it seems endless."

"It's more than endless. But it's the power. It's the most addictive feeling I've ever had. The more anger I have, the more revenge I want."

38

TO HELL YOU RIDE

Chopper Town Biker Bar

"Gears," said one of the other bikers as he stared at a television screen. The flicker of light from the TV popped across his face. "You'll wanna take a look at this." The burly man held a pool cue with both hands and leaned his face against it. His bloodshot eyes told the tale of a long night of drinking. He looked behind himself. In the early morning hours, the biker bar had finally descended into relative calm. When no one answered, he looked over his shoulder at the pool table where Gears Pliskin was laid out. "Pliskin!" he said, a little louder this time. "Dammit."

He tossed the pool cue onto a table and walked to the next one over. He shook Gears until his eyes cracked open.

"What in hell do you want?" Pliskin said, his voice

husky. "You wake up a man, you better be prepared to pay the price."

"Come on, Gears. Get up. You gotta come see this. Something happened."

"Happened?" Pliskin said as he sat upright. "Somethin's about to happen, to your skull, that is."

"No, look." He pointed at the TV monitor where a helicopter-mounted camera pointed down at the remains of a ramshackle house. The house was surrounded by police cruisers and fire trucks. Smoke still poured from the structure and fire crews sprayed water from three different sides. "Ain't that the hangout? You know, the local shithole our patches use."

Pliskin rubbed sleep from his eyes and squinted. "Well, fuck me sideways. Damn thing burned to the ground. And what's the heat all over the place for?"

"You don't think the feds already chased down the screw ups from that bank robbery, do you?" the patch asked.

"Hell if I know," Pliskin said. He stared at the screen. "Turn up that volume. How did that place burn down?"

As the two listened to the newscast, Pliskin could hardly believe what he was hearing.

The camera view on the TV switched to a reporter on the ground, a young pretty blonde who held a microphone and spoke. "Fire crews continue to fight the four-alarm blaze here, Dave. Yet no one knows what started the fire in this house, a known criminal hangout, or at least they aren't saying. But the level of police activity is highly unusual and suggests that perhaps foul play is involved. Over there," she said as she pointed at an official vehicle parked in the distance, "that's the office of the coroner, and fire inspectors have begun to arrive as well."

"Are police commenting further, Tammy?" the anchor back at the KHOU news station asked.

"The only thing they've said, Dave, is that at least thirty victims are inside. And if you look, though it's hard to see from this vantage point, you can just see the handlebars from dozens of motorcycles. Those motorcycles belonged to someone, and what's feared is that their owners are all deceased. We'll keep you up to speed as the facts emerge. For now, I'm Tammy Lightner, KHOU Channel Eleven news, with weather, traffic and sports on the hour."

As the news program switched back to the news desk, Gears Pliskin hopped off the pool table where he had been sleeping.

"Holy shit. The boss is sure gonna be pissed about this."

The other biker picked up his pool cue and lined up a shot. "That's why I woke you up. *I* sure as hell ain't going to tell him."

39

THE UPDATE

Pearland Police Department

"Whelan, get your ass in here and give me an update," the police captain yelled.

"Thirty fatalities. Charred to bits."

"How do you plan on identifying them?"

"Already done."

"Oh bullshit. How did you identify thirty charred bodies?"

"Their bikes. Thirty dead thugs, thirty Harley's out front. It took a while, but believe it or not, they were registered legally. I guess biker types take their street bikes seriously. But, several of them had switched license plates. We were able to pull the VIN numbers and get proper identities of the owners though. From there, we'll try to match dental records to corpses."

"So, who are they?"

"Like we thought. All members of our favorite biker gang, the Lincoln Killers."

The captain thought about that a moment. "There were still thirty members locally, even after that guy capped seven of them?"

"That's right, captain. But a few were from other states. Apparently, their national organization took an interest in the upcoming trial. It should start on Monday."

"You don't sound so confident. The trial's not starting?"

"Oh, it'll start all right, but without the star witness. The victim, Peyton Phoenix, made it clear she wasn't going to testify."

"Well, who can blame her?"

"The trial isn't the interesting part," Whelan said.

"Are you going to tell me, or am I going to have to jump over this desk and kick your ass?"

"Most of the bikers didn't die in the fire."

There was silence.

Lt. Whelan continued, "They were shot. Well, shot or blown to bits."

"Are you fucking kidding me?" the captain said as he stood. "You're telling me thirty armed thugs were shot or blown up? Who the hell could kill thirty guys?"

"It was a professional hit. I spoke to the Fire Marshall. He said there's no doubt, some type of white phosphorous accelerant was all over the place. And most victims had either one shot to the center forehead, or a double-tap, center mass. The shot groupings are tight as hell. And in each case, it wasn't just a kill-shot."

"What else?"

"Each of those vics was shot in the balls."

"Bullshit!"

"Each had no more than four rounds in them. Most had only two. The ones with two had one to the forehead, one to the nuts. The others had two to center mass, one to the forehead, and one to the nuts. We're presuming those were double tapped in the chest first, followed up with a kill shot to the head. But, every single one of them is shot in the crown jewels. I'm telling you, we're talking about a professional hit on a whole different scale."

"Oh, the media is going to have a field day with this." The captain's face sank into his hands. "Any witnesses?"

"Nothing yet, but the uni's are still combing the area." Whelan was holding back information, and he knew it. "Do you remember what I said the night the Phoenix woman was attacked?"

"No."

"I told you this guy, this Terminator guy, was something else. I told you he was special ops, a covert operative, Navy SEAL, something. And you looked at me like I was a jackass."

The captain stood and was about to bark something, but Whelan was having none of it.

"I told you then, and I'll tell you now!" Whelan yelled.

"We're dealing with a highly trained individual. Nobody is equipped with the kind of training it would take to do this except the military. He's black ops for sure."

"Bullshit," the captain said.

"Look, captain, I'm right about this. I'm right, and I don't give a flying fuck if you don't believe me. We're looking for a black-ops-trained assassin. One that's gone fucking crazy or something. And so far, we've got nothing to go on."

"All right, all right. But one thing doesn't add up. Lieutenant." The last word rolled off the captain's tongue like it tasted of vinegar. "If we're talking about some hot-shit covert assassin who's run amuck, then why did he shoot them in the balls? Maybe I can buy the assassin angle, but I don't see a man shooting thirty dudes in the nuts."

"I haven't worked that part out yet. Maybe he's taking revenge on the Lincoln Killer gang for attacking Peyton Phoenix."

"Uh huh," the captain said as he crossed his arms. "And what about the witness who stated he saw a woman leaving the scene?"

Whelan paused a moment. "You know about that?"

"What do you think I am? A jackass? I know everything that goes on in this place. So, what about it? Sounds to me like maybe it is this Phoenix woman. Maybe she got pissed off about being attacked and took it out on her attackers."

"Boss, there's no way. I've met her, remember? She's five foot nothing and couldn't weigh one hundred and ten pounds, soaking wet."

The captain's eyes narrowed, and he leaned closed fists

onto his desk. "Well, whoever the woman is, a female meeting her description apparently walked out just before the fire erupted. That makes her a person of interest."

Whelan rubbed his eyes. "I know."

"Then get on it! And get that Phoenix woman in here for questioning. I want to know her whereabouts at the time of the murders. I say, she's your doer. Not to mention the fact that if her life wasn't in danger yesterday, it damn sure is now. One way or another, she needs protection. If those bikers think that this has anything to do with the attack on Phoenix, they'll send every swinging dick they have left at her. They'll interpret this the same as we did, that one way or another, this was revenge for the attack on Peyton Phoenix."

"There's something else," Whelan said as he continued rubbing both eyes.

"Well spit it out, dammit."

Whelan looked up. "Peyton Phoenix disappeared."

"What?"

"Three weeks ago," Whelan said. "We went to check on her after the bank robbery. Her coworkers said she had vanished right before it went down. We figured she just went into hiding, but I don't know anymore. Normally if somebody up and hauls ass, they still have ways of communicating with their friends or family. In this case, Ms. Phoenix hasn't even reached out to her mother to let her know she's still alive."

"That doesn't sound good. You think she was kidnapped?"

"I don't know. Maybe. Maybe she was killed, and this Terminator guy is taking revenge on the bikers. All the district attorney said was they tried for weeks to get her to agree to testify, but she refused them all along. Then she up and vanished."

"Wait just a god damned minute," the captain said as he walked around the front of his desk. "You're telling me she disappeared? That was her bank branch that was just robbed, and two people were murdered. And she just happened to not be there that day?"

"I don't know, lucky break I guess."

"Lucky break?" the captain said. "Maybe those were gang members who robbed the bank and were really coming after her. Maybe she found out about it in advance and got the hell out of there."

"Captain, she said she wasn't going to testify. That was just a bank robbery gone bad, plain and simple. Besides, since she wasn't going to testify, why would there be a need for the Lincoln Killers to kill her?"

"Whelan, these bikers don't think like you and I do. They have no remorse, they have no thought process, for that matter. These are purebred thugs, through and through. They'd just want to tie off all the loose ends, just in case. You know what I think, Lieutenant? I think you're too close to this thing. I think you're blind to the fact that she has every reason to want to kill those gang members. That's *motivation* in my book. Probable cause."

"The thirty dead bodies are the work of a trained assassin, and I intend to find him."

"Him?" the captain said as he returned to his chair and began writing on a document. "I want that Phoenix woman found, and I want her brought in here for questioning."

Whelan walked out. The captain stood and yelled for him. "Whelan? Whelan?"

40

NEWS BREAKS

A news report broke into the regularly scheduled programming.

"WBS News, with weather, traffic and sports. This is breaking news. Updating the story we told you about earlier in which thirty bodies were recovered after a horrific house fire. Unconfirmed sources now tell us that the thirty victims did not die in the fire. For more, we turn to our correspondent in the field, Tammy Lightner. Tammy, what can you tell us?"

"Well John, we've just spoken with fire authorities here at the scene, and it now appears that the victims all show signs of multiple gunshot wounds. If that can be confirmed, it would mean this is not the largest mass casualty event as the result of a fire, but the largest mass homicide in state history. At this time, police and federal authorities remain silent on the subject, but speculation is swirling at this hour—"

Will turned the radio off. "Well, it's all over the airways now. Shit, they'll put the feds on this one for sure. We'll have FBI swarming all over the place. So, what do you think of your little rampage now, missy?"

Peyton looked at Will with steel in her eyes. "I say, fuck them. I already told you. They got what was coming to them."

"Peyton," Brock said, "this is serious. Will and I have been talking. We've got to get out of here. Sooner or later they'll find out what happened. They always do. And when that happens we need to be far away from here."

She stared into the cold darkness outside. "I'm not going anywhere."

"What do you mean by that?" Will questioned. "We're in this together."

"Peyton, please," Brock injected. "We've got to go on the run. They'll catch us otherwise. And Will is right. Look, I love you. I mean that more than I think I've ever meant it. I love you and I don't want to see you hurt. But worse, I don't want to see this eat you from the inside out, like it did me. Killing people has a way of doing that. But for now, we've got to preserve what we can. We move out in an hour."

"You go. Both of you. I've got something left to do. I'll do this alone if I have to. I'm not leaving."

Brock's brow furled. "What do you mean, you've got something left to do?"

"He wasn't there," Peyton said.

"Who wasn't there?" Brock replied.

She clenched her jaw. "The one survivor."

"Wait," Brock said. "You mean the one that didn't die in the hospital? One of your original attackers?"

"Damn right," Peyton said. She rubbed her temples and her breathing deepened.

Will shook his head. "You'll get yourself killed is what you'll do, little lady."

"I want him dead," she said. "I want them all dead. But I'm not leaving without his head on a stick."

Brock rubbed his eyes. "There's too much heat. He's rotting in some jail cell. What do you want to do, walk into a police precinct and start shooting?"

Peyton's voice exploded. "I'm going to kill him if it's the last thing I do!"

"It will be the last thing you'll do!" Brock yelled back.

"Don't you see what's happening?" Peyton said. "He wasn't there when I killed the rest of them. I admit, I didn't even think about that. Now, the Lincoln Killers gang will flock here. They'll be all over the place. In every biker bar this side of Louisiana. It'll be easy pickings. But I will kill every one of those sons of a bitches."

Brock held her. "You've lost it. Don't do this. I can't stand it. You're going to get yourself killed."

"Even if I do, it will be worth it. I'm not the same frightened girl you first met. I don't feel that anymore. I don't feel anything anymore. All I know is, I can't rest knowing that that any of those pricks are still out there. You know what they're like, right? They'll be down here, getting in fights, groping women, attacking some of them. I'll not stand for it.

No more. It stops here. It stops now. If I have the power, I'll kill them all."

Will walked to Brock and whispered, "We're never going to talk her down. I say we drug her and throw her in the RV, then get out of here. When she wakes up, we'll all be a long way from here."

"What was that?" Peyton asked.

"Give us a second, Peyton," Brock said as he pulled Will out onto the porch. "We're not going to drug her," Brock said. "But I've been thinking. Now that she went all postal, even if we try to drive out of here, those bikers will be flooding in from all sides. Anywhere we go we're likely to be seen. I don't want a full-on firefight. You and I live under the radar. Nobody even knows we exist. I'm not about to give that up. No, I say we stay put. And besides, Will, look at her. She reminds me of me when I first started. You're a hell of a lot older—"

"Watch it," Will said.

"And you'd probably say the same thing about yourself when you first started. At first everything feels so cold, so ice-like. Then, eventually it all settles into your gut and you suddenly realize what you've done. And then everything feels unreal. It's only then that she'll calm down. But look at her, man. She's fucking perfect. She's the most beautiful, most perfect assassin I've ever seen. I say, we get her back on the plan of using her body to lure out one biker at a time. They're easier to control like that."

Will rubbed his eyes. "You want to keep killing them?"

"What choice do we have? We both know they're going

to find out soon enough, and when they do, they're going to come after us. We need to thin out their numbers while we still have the tactical advantage. And besides, if we can kill the last one, the one that attacked her, we can convince her to leave."

Will put his hands on his hips. "How in the hell do I let you talk me into such messes?"

Brock laughed. "Because you've got the I.Q. of a common house plant." They walked back inside. He looked at Peyton. "Let's sit down and talk about this thing. Peyton, come over to the table." Once they were seated, Brock laid down his plans. "Listen, we're with you, okay? We aren't going to leave you alone. We're all in this together. But if Will and I are going to help, we're in charge here." Peyton started to protest but he held up his hand. "No. That's the way it's going to be. Will and I have operational experience. You can't have an operation where orders aren't followed. I mean that, Peyton. I'm in charge."

Her eyes capitulated. "Want me under your control, huh?" She peeled a little grin and said, "That's not what's been happening in bed."

Will rolled his eyes. "Alright, I don't need to know what goes on in the sack between the two of you. But come to think of it, Brock, if she's taken charge in there, you need to man-up."

"Oh, shut up," Brock laughed. "So here's what I have in mind. Peyton, we're going to do some surveillance on one of the likely biker bars that we'd find some targets. Particularly that last survivor. The gang members will be easy to spot with those stupid leather vests. I'll set up on a rooftop across from the bar. You'll go in and lure one of them out. Just one, I don't want too many loose cannons. Once you've lured him outside, I'll take him down with the sniper rifle. I'll use the silencer so no one will even hear the shot."

Peyton shifted in her seat as the thought of taking out another made her smile. Brock noticed the effect his talking about killing was having on Peyton. He cleared his throat.

"Like I was saying, we'll pick out our spots carefully. We'll have full visibility so there'll be no surprises. Will, you'll be close by, cocked, locked and ready to rock. You'll be there in case there's any trouble, both during the time Peyton's in the bar, and after she brings one of them out."

"Roger that."

"And, if all goes well, Will, you'll need to drag off the body into the darkness somewhere, and we'll reload and try to lure another one out." He looked Peyton dead in the eyes. "And we'll kill another one of those sons of bitches."

"We've got work to do," Will said.

But Brock stood, then picked up Peyton and carried her into the bedroom. The last intelligible words Will overheard was Brock saying, "Don't think I'm in charge in the bedroom, huh?"

Will heard a giggle.

COMING FOR HER

Chopper Town Biker Bar

"Grinder? You got a minute?" Gears said as he stood facing the gang president

Grinder looked up through thick sunglasses. He picked up a long neck bottle of Budweiser and tossed it back. When it was empty, he grabbed at the next. He wiped his lip, and dried blood met the back of his hand. He looked at the crusty, dark blood and grinned. "That was a good 'un. Last night, I mean. Kicked that redneck's ass, didn't we?" He laughed. "Got a minute? Damn, Gears, you think we work in an office?" He laughed harder and this time nudged a sleeping gang member beside him. When the man didn't move, he said, "Ha. Look at him. No wonder we call him Baby-Face. Spit it out, dammit.

"It ain't good, boss."

"What is it this time? One of our boys get into a scrape with a local patch again? Damn, I told them boys, just because you see me do it, don't give you the right. We wear the same colors, don't we? It ain't that hard of a rule to follow."

"No, that's not it. Something has happened. It's all over the news."

"Shit, you mean them boys we had do the bank robbery got pinched?"

"No, worse. Much worse. The news is reporting that thirty of our guys got killed in a fire at the hangout. The place is burned to the ground. All their choppers are still outside. It doesn't look like any of them made it out."

"What are you talking about?" Grinder said through a slight chuckle. When he found a beer bottle with an inch of swill at the bottom, he tossed it back, then shook his head. "Ain't nobody dead. Not yet, at least."

"Boss, no, it's like I said. The news is on every channel. There are cops everywhere. They're saying it's the biggest mass murder in state history."

"Murder? Bullshit. You mean to tell me somebody killed our boys? That's bull fucking shit. That's what that is." But as he stared at Gears, his facial expression flattened. He yanked the shades off his eyes and stood. His motion was so abrupt, he bumped the table and bottles tipped over and fell to the ground, some breaking in the process. "They're dead?" he said. His voice had turned to acid. "Fucking dead?" He paced the floor then spun back around and stood

within an inch of Gear's face. "Nobody could kill all those guys."

"They interviewed one of the feds outside the hangout. Said everybody he covered had multiple gunshot wounds. They probably started the fire just to cover their tracks."

"Whoever did this is dead!"

"One other thing. We got a guy on the payroll. Works at the local police precinct as a janitor or some shit. Anyway, he's on the up. Called in this morning to say that the cops had a witness that saw a woman come walking out of there just before he saw smoke."

Grinder turned his back and scanned the far end of the bar as one looking for something that wasn't there. Then, in a slow whisper, he uttered words that not even Gears could hear. "You fucking bitch. I'm coming for you."

A SINGLE PHONE CALL

The Cabin

As the sun rose, Brock started to stir. He heard faint sounds coming from the main room of the cabin. It sounded like the dull clank of metal on metal. But he was still in a state of sleep deprivation, so he gave himself a moment to process the sounds. They sounded simply like Peyton and Will making breakfast.

When his feet hit the cool wooden floor planks, he located his boxer shorts and got dressed. But when he walked into the main room, he saw only Peyton. She wasn't making breakfast. Instead, she was speaking into a cellphone.

"And I'm coming for you next," she said, then hung up the phone.

"What was that?" Brock said as a scowl formed on his face.

"Nothing."

"Nothing? It didn't sound like nothing." He rubbed sleep from his eyes. "Tell me the truth."

But Peyton walked out the cabin's front door.

Will walked from his bedroom into the kitchen and pulled a bag of roasted coffee beans out of the cabinet. He glanced at Brock who was standing there. "You're just about worthless, aren't you?"

Brock reached down and picked up the cellphone, then looked at the screen. He turned it so Will could see and said, "You recognize this number?"

"No, why?" But Will set the coffee beans down and stared again at the number. "Wait a minute." Will walked back into his room, then emerged with a manila file folder. He leafed through the contents. "Wait just a god damned minute. Someone has been in this folder."

"What is it?"

"Intel," was all he said. He stared at Brock and his jaw muscles flexed.

"Intel?" Brock let the thoughts play forward in his mind a moment. "Intel on the Lincoln Killers?"

"Well, it sure as shit isn't intel on that Chang Kai Chen target we did in Surinam."

"If that's intel on the Lincoln Killers . . ."

"Yeah," Will barked. "She rifled through the file. That phone number? That's the personal cell number of one

Michael John Brewer. AKA, *Grinder*. A friend of mine at the Bureau pulled it for me."

"Fuck me."

"No shit," Will said as he slapped the file folder down onto the table. "She fucking did it. She called the president of the Lincoln Killers gang."

Brock pulled a chair back and sat. "She's crazier than I thought."

"Where is she?"

"Just went out. Grabbed her carbine and is probably going for a run on the trails."

"This is unacceptable, compadre. We're in deep kimchee now. When I signed up for this, I wasn't thinking of committing suicide. Fucking-A, Brock. What is she thinking?"

Brock's hands went across the back of his neck. "Off the reservation. Gone completely off the reservation. She's just signed our death warrants."

"Ha," Will replied. "She signed those yesterday when she executed thirty gang members from an organization that probably has ten thousand."

"I know what she's done," Brock said.

"Let's grab her and get the hell out of here."

"She'll never stand for that now. She's gotten a taste for it, and she's not going to stop until she's satisfied."

"Oh, that's just fucking great, compadre. She's out of control? Is that what you're saying? We can't hold her here, can't get her to leave? Is that it?"

Brock exhaled. "That's exactly what I'm saying. She'll

fight us, she'll sneak off and go after them alone. And I can't stand by and watch that. I can't."

"We're trapped now," Will said as he shook his head. His volume escalated. "There's so much heat in the area, and bikers coming in from all directions. Hell, the only thing we can do is quietly try and pick off a couple of them. Maybe if we do that, we can get her out of here. But let me tell you something. If we get out of this alive, we're getting her far away from here."

"But that's not all, is it? I know you too well, Will. Spit it out."

"No, it's not all. If we get out of this mess, I'm out of it. I came back because you needed help. But if you're going to run off and kill yourself, you can damn well do it without me."

43

THE SETUP

Two hours later, Peyton came back into the cabin. The AR-15 was slung over her back, and she was drenched in sweat. Still breathing heavily from her exhaustive run, she looked at Brock. His back was to her as he stared out the expansive sliding glass doors. He did not turn around.

Peyton knew he was stewing. "I don't want to talk about it," she said.

"Well, you're going to talk about it." He turned and looked at her, his arms crossed.

"I don't have time for this." She marched toward the one restroom. "I'm jumping in the shower."

He walked in front of her and blocked her path. "You don't get to just make this shit up as you go, particularly without consulting us."

"It's my life, Brock."

"No, it's not. Will and I, our lives are on the line too. The three of us are a team, and you just put the entire team in jeopardy. All because you've got this fucked up notion that killing anyone wearing a Lincoln Killers patch on his back will make you feel better. I've got news for you, it doesn't work that way."

She tried to push him aside, but he stood firm. "It does work that way. I feel more alive than I have in a long time. And I'll tell you something else, I *enjoyed* killing them."

"You have no idea what you've gotten yourself into. Once it sinks in, it's going to haunt you for the rest of your life."

"That's bullshit!" she barked. She turned and walked to the kitchen table, slung the rifle off her back and disassembled it, placing each part on the table in order.

"You think that's it, then?" He walked toward her. "That you can just take human life, and there are no consequences? Let me tell you from direct experience, there *are* consequences. It changes you. It changes you permanently." He threw his hands into the air. "Jesus Christ, Phoenix, in all the ops I ever went on, even I haven't killed thirty people."

She turned, and her eyes narrowed to slits. "I am not you. And I don't feel a thing. Tonight, when I lay down, I'll sleep like a baby. Those pricks don't deserve another thought."

Will walked in from the other bedroom and shook his head. "I see you two are at it again."

Brock glanced at Will but then turned to Peyton. "You called the president of the Lincoln Killers gang, didn't you?"

"I sure as hell did," she replied. "And I told him I was coming for him."

Will flopped onto the couch.

Brock said, "You told him you were coming for him? Are you insane?"

"No, I'm not insane. I know exactly what I'm doing and why. In fact, for the first time in my life, everything makes sense to me." She glanced between Brock and Will, then said, "I'm going to take down their national president and anyone near him. And I'm going to enjoy myself. That means with or without the two of you."

Will draped an arm over the couch. "Might as well go along with it, Compadre," he said to Brock. "Shit, man, the only way out of this thing now is to kill the rest of them. Otherwise, we'll never stop looking over our shoulders. Hell, maybe if we kill their president, it will disorganize them, and the rest will scatter. Otherwise, we'll always think that we're being watched or followed. We'll never be able to start a car or motorcycle again without wondering if it's rigged to explode."

"Cut off the head, huh?" Brock replied.

"Just like that job we did in Bangkok. Once we took out that militia leader, the rest fled to the jungle."

Brock's shoulders slumped, and he shook his head.

Peyton walked to him. "Come on, baby. It's the only way."

"I guess you two leave me no choice. But if we do this, we do it *my* way. Do you hear me? The only way Will and I survived all those missions was because we planned every last thing. You can't go off half-cocked and decide to do whatever you want." He towered over her. "Am I understood?"

"All right, all right," she replied.

Although her voice was sheepish, there was fire in her eyes.

Brock turned and walked out onto the balcony. He placed his hands on the rail and stared out at the beauty of nature. He let out a long exhale and knew, trouble awaited them.

44

COPS

Pearland Police Department

As two men in crisp, dark business suits walked into the captain's office, Whelan looked up from his desk. He squinted to focus on the men, but then glanced back at his laptop.

"Feds. Damn, those guys are so arrogant," a younger, plain-clothed detective sitting at the adjacent desk said.

Whelan didn't look up. "You're too young to be jaded already, Danny."

"What are you working on, L.T.?"

"Huh? Oh, sorry. Just a bit preoccupied with the thirty files on my desk. Christ, up until this point, I've covered a total of thirty bodies in my career. That's twelve years of homicides in this area. Now, in one fell swoop, another thirty drop into my lap."

"Damn glad I'm not you. But wait a minute. That doesn't sound like you. I mean, I know your desk is covered in corpses right now, but something wrong?"

"You ask a lot of questions. What are you, a cop?" The levity went nowhere. "Is something wrong?" Whelan said as he exhaled. "No. Yes. Shit, I don't know," Whelan ran fingers through his hair to push it off his forehead. "Something else happened." Whelan looked over his shoulder to see if anyone was within earshot. "Can you keep a secret?"

The detective nodded.

"Turns out that one of the uni's had a witness. Some guy was outside at the shopping center just after the shootings went down. He saw someone walking from the scene."

"Holy shit, did he get a good look at the guy?"

"That's just it, it wasn't a guy. It was a woman. He just said she was Caucasian, trim, light brown hair, but couldn't really see anything else."

"Well, at least it's something. But you and I both know it couldn't have been a woman. So, what are you thinking?"

Whelan looked up. "She's likely one of the biker chicks. Probably saw the whole thing happen, but once it was over, she got the hell out of there."

"Definitely someone we'd want to talk to."

"No doubt," Whelan replied. "Thing is, the captain has this hairbrained idea that our doer is female. He thinks the fact that all these guys were shot in the balls is a dead giveaway."

"That Phoenix woman, the victim?"

"Right. But I say that's crap. Our perp is an ex-military guy, the one that came to her rescue the night she was attacked. This was his work."

"Whelan?" the captain yelled from his office door. "Need you to step in here for a minute."

Whelan rolled his eyes. "What does he want now?"

"Looks like the feds want a word with you."

"Yeah," Whelan said, they probably want to do this as a joint task force so that once I nab the perp, they can take credit and get their faces on the news."

Danny laughed. "You've got a great attitude, you know that? You're my role model."

Whelan stood and began walking toward the office. "Set your sights a little higher, kid."

45

INTEL GATHERED

The Cabin

The trio sat at the kitchen table and spread out a paper map. "You have the rest of those bikers still at that shithole bar?" Brock said as he pointed at a spot on the map.

Will replied, "Yep. Trailed them out there last night. Got a friend, works the night shift. Said they were there all night. Got rowdy as hell."

"No doubt. So, what else is at this crossroads?"

"Right across and diagonal is a two-story, an old hardware store. Perfect sniper's nest. Have a great view of two sides."

"Which two sides?"

"The left side of the building, with a view straight down the building where the back door is."

"What's in the back?" Brock asked.

"Not much back there. Just a dumpster. No lighting or anything. Be a perfect place for me to be."

Brock nodded. "Night-vision scope should do well then."

"Ahem," Peyton said, purposely interrupting. Both men looked at her. "You two just going to plan this entire op without me?"

"Like I said, Peyton," Brock replied, "we do this my way, and we plan every detail, every contingency."

"It isn't going to be that hard," she said as she leaned back. "First, I'll dye my hair. Since my face looks different after all the surgeries, between that and the different hair color, they'll never recognize me. I'll walk in and get one of them interested in going outside for a little ooo-la-la. It'll be late, they'll all be drunk, as usual. And it won't just be dark outside, it'll be dark inside that place as well. They won't suspect a thing. I'll bring them out the back door. It will be perfect. I can use the silencer on the .380. One shot to the head and they'll crumple into a pile of their own piss and vomit."

"Easy?" Will said as he stood. "Listen, killing is never easy. It takes planning. Anything can happen."

"He's right," Brock said, a little more sternly than he had intended. "Things go wrong. Your weapon can jam, an extra can show up."

"An extra person?" Peyton said with a smile. "Then I just take them both out."

"You're lucky we're letting you do this at all," Brock barked. "It's our asses on the line too. You go inside, pull out one, and I'll take him down with the rifle. It'll be fitted with a silencer as well, and we can just let the bodies pile up in the darkness. That'll be our best defense, to reduce their numbers, so we have a chance to skin out of here."

"Jesus," Peyton said as she stood. "It's like talking to a bunch of old ladies. All right, fine, I'll bring one out at a time, and you can drop them. In fact, it might be fun to watch."

Will shook his head. "I don't like this. Not enough intel, no backup, no extraction, outnumbered ten to one."

"I hear you, brother," Brock said. "Let's just get through this and get the hell out of here." He looked at Peyton. "You. You're the wildcard here. Do we understand each other? You bring one them out one at a time. There are at least thirty of them left. If we can cut their numbers in half, we stand a fighting chance of getting out of this should we got caught in a firefight. This has got to be done quietly. Nothing we do can draw their attention, or the game is up."

She held her hand in a salute position, "Yes, sir." Though Peyton had no intention of doing this quietly.

46

THE COMPANY

Pearland Police Department

Whelan walked into the captain's office. The captain stood behind his desk and motioned for Whelan to close the door behind him. He pointed to the two suits.

"Whelan, you know Special Agent Wilmont, Bureau."

Wilmont stood, nodded to Whelan, and shook his hand.

The captain continued. "And this is Lawrence Wallace. He's with . . . another agency."

The man's face was pockmarked, as if it had been scarred by being dragged across gravel. Whelan leaned toward the man with his hand extended, but Wallace remained seated, one leg crossed over the other. He did not acknowledge Whelan. Instead, he glanced at his crisp suit trousers and swept a hand across a piece of lint.

"Yeah, nice to make your acquaintance too," Whelan said as he rolled his eyes.

"Mr. Wallace has some information he'd like to share with you."

"*Mister* Wallace?" Whelan said. "And he's with *another* agency? Uh huh." Whelan knew Wallace was CIA. "So, what does the Company have to do with a mass murder investigation?"

Wallace looked only at the captain. "Like I said." His voice was harsh, like that of a person with damaged vocal cords caused by years of yelling. "You've got a bit of a situation on your hands, so let me help you. The man you're after is named Brock Paladin." He withdrew a black and white photograph from a leather attaché and flicked it across the captain's desk.

Whelan leaned across the desk and squinted at the photo. He looked at Wallace and said, "What makes you so sure this is our doer?"

Wallace cleared his throat but ignored the question. "Mr. Paladin is what we call a wet boy."

"Paladin is an assassin, then?" Whelan said.

"That's putting it lightly," Wallace replied. "In Paladin's case, he's more like a predator. When he worked for us, he was known as The Caiman, named after the crocodile of the Amazon Basin. He was successful, very successful. And apparently, he's now come into a bit of a disagreement with the Lincoln Killers motorcycle gang."

"A disagreement?" Whelan said. "Whoever did this had

more than a passing disagreement with them. I've got thirty bodies in the morgue."

Wallace looked at Whelan for the first time. "It was a figure of speech. At any rate, he disappeared a couple of years ago. Damn shame, too. The Caiman was the best there is."

"Oh really?" Whelan said as his face reddened. "What did he used to do for you? Assassinate heads of state, run heroin to the rebels, topple regimes so you could insert someone friendly to the US?"

"Whelan!" the captain said. "Sit down."

Whelan stared at Wallace, his jaw muscles clenching.

The captain looked at Wallace. "We'll need a full dossier on this Brock Paladin, Mr. Wallace. And we need it all. No holding back."

Wallace swept his hand across his trousers again. "What I've given you is already more than I should have. There is no dossier, gentlemen. Mr. Paladin's background is classified."

Whelan slammed both fists onto the captain's desk. "Screw you, and your god damned wet boys, Wallace."

"Whelan!" the captain yelled again.

Whelan said, "You're not going to help us, then why the hell are you here?"

Wallace grinned at him, as one who takes pleasure in the misfortunes of others. "It was a professional courtesy."

Before Whelan could launch at him, the captain stood. He held an arm in front of Whelan and pushed him toward the door. "Lieutenant Whelan is right, Mr. Wallace. We're investigating murder, and the federal government has no right to withhold state's evidence."

Wallace stood and was followed by Special Agent Wilmont. Wallace walked to Whelan and extended a hand. "No hard feelings." When Whelan did not reciprocate, Wallace walked out.

As Agent Wilmont passed, he said, "Sorry about that. The guy can be a real asshole."

Whelan looked at him. "You have to go to Quantico to learn that?"

Wilmont shook his head and left.

Whelan started to walk out but turned. "There you have it. I told you we were looking for an assassin."

"Hey," the captain barked, "this is our jurisdiction. Just because some CIA prick comes in here and says he knows who's responsible don't mean shit in this office. I still say the Phoenix woman is a person of interest, and I want her brought in. She's good for it, and you know it."

"You've been doing this too long, captain. The heat's gone to your head." Whelan walked out.

47

FIND HER!

Chopper Town Biker Bar

Michael John Brewer picked a round table off the floor, raised it over his head and threw it through the plate glass window at the front of the bar. "I want that bitch found!" he yelled over the shattering glass.

"Come on, boss, it's me," Gears said. "I've got every swinging dick available combing the area. Hell, the only Harley's you see sitting out there are mine and yours. Everybody else is gone. They'll find her."

The bartender, a burly, barrel-chested man with a gargantuan beard walked around. He held a stubby wooden bat in his hand. "Hey! You mother fuckers broke my window." He poked Grinder in the chest with it. "Look, I don't give a shit that you got the biggest, baddest biker gang in the world. This is *my* place. I'll kill every last one of you."

"You got a problem with us, do you?" Grinder said.

Gears interposed himself in between Grinder and the bartender. "Boss, cool it, man. This dude doesn't have anything to do with the girl. Besides, you just broke his six-hundred-dollar window. We got too much at stake, and damn sure don't need the law descending on us right now."

The bartender's chest heaved.

"Fine," Grinder said. "Pay the man for the window."

Gears pulled out a wad of cash to quiet the bartender.

The man took the cash and shook his head. "Now I got to clean this shit up and call the damn window guy. Third time this month. Might as well add it to the menu." He pointed the bat at the chalkboard menu behind the bar. "Budweiser Pitchers, Budweiser Long Necks, Hamburger, Cheeseburger, Fries, Ten-foot glass window." He counted his cash and walked off to go get a broom.

"Boss, it's almost dark. Those boys are gonna start piling back in here, and if they don't have the girl, you gotta deal with it."

"Don't tell me what to do," Grinder spit back. "I'm just telling you, I want that bitch found."

Gears motioned to a table where the men sat. "I got guys going down every back road in the area. I got 'em covering the only roads out of here too. Man, I'm telling you, she ain't getting past us."

"She'd better not. That cunt thinks she can threaten me, I'll cut her in half."

"Don't worry," Gears said. "I'm personally on this. You just sit tight. Right now, I'm going to head out and go check on the guys watching the roads. Just want to make sure nobody's sleeping on the job. You'll see. We'll get her."

48

ALL POINTS

Pearland Police Department

"So, L.T.," Danny, the young plainclothes detective said, "what's the play?"

Whelan looked at him as he put the vehicle in reverse. "I figure it like this. We've got to find that Phoenix woman."

"Yeah, from what the captain said, she's the doer."

"Bullshit!" Whelan barked as he accelerated hard enough that the tires squealed. "Our doer is that CIA boy, Brock Paladin. I've met Peyton Phoenix, and I'm telling you, she ain't got it in her. But Paladin, for whatever reason, he's really got a thing for these bikers. From looking at his photo, he's a match for the Terminator guy from the bar, that night Peyton Phoenix was attacked. No, we need to find the woman just to get her out of harm's way. Not to mention that she can corroborate that Paladin is the doer. She's our star witness. He's got the training, he's apparently pretty pissed off with the Lincoln Killers, and he's never not completed a mission."

"A mission? L.T., he's not working a covert assignment."

"No, he's not. But you heard that CIA asshole, Lawrence Wallace. Brock Paladin never failed. The way I see it, he has no intention of failing this time."

"If we haven't found the Phoenix woman up to this point, how do you intend to find her now?"

"We find the rest of the Lincoln Killers, we'll find Paladin. Either they'll lead us to him or vice versa. There's only a handful of biker bars in the area. I figure we'll drive by each of them, run a few plates off of a few of the Harley's out front, and we'll know if we're in the right place or not."

Danny tilted his head. "You're the boss, boss."

49

ROOFTOP ADVANTAGE

Chopper Town Biker Bar

By midnight, the place was hopping. Music blared from speakers, and most of the bikers had a longneck in their hands. Half of them were already wobbling in various states of inebriation. At a table on the side of the bar, one held up a tiny Ziplock baggie and flicked it. White powder emptied from the bag. He took out a razor and cut the cocaine into four neat rows, then pulled out a straw. He snorted one line, then handed the straw to the next.

* * *

Outside, the air was crisp as Brock, Will, and Peyton drove up behind the building adjacent to the bar. The headlights had already been doused as Will pulled the vehicle to a stop and cut the engine. "We're in Indian country now," he said. He turned and grinned at Peyton. "Sure, you don't want to just keep driving?"

"Not a chance," she said. "Besides, you saw when we drove by that they're at least ten Harley's short. The others are still camped out, watching the roads."

"I hate this," Brock said. "She's right. If we tried to slip away, we'd be seen for sure. One of them would call the others, and it would be like a swarm of hornets coming down on us."

Will's eyes glazed over and he stared out into the blackness. "We've been in worse scrapes before. We've got the firepower. I prefer a straight-on fight to all this sneaking around crap."

"The plan is laid, Will," Brock said.

"I know it is. All right, while you get set up on the roof, I'll use the time to swing around through the woods and come up behind the place." He looked at Peyton. "When you start pulling those guys out the back door, I'll be right there, twenty feet away, just inside the tree line. Make sure you stay out of the line of fire between you and Brock. Brock's job is to take them down. My job is to be your backup in case this goes sideways."

"Stay out of the line of fire. Got it," she said.

Will stood, went to the back of the RV and withdrew his AR-15 rifle and comms headset. He placed the comm link into his ear, checked the chamber on the rifle, then raised the rifle to his shoulder. He glanced through the night-vision scope until he was satisfied. "Check, check," he said into the mic.

"Got you," Brock replied after donning his comms unit.

Will threw a pack over his back and raised a hand to Brock, Urban style. They shook. "You watch your ass, compadre," Will said.

Brock's brow furled. "What's wrong?" he asked.

"Last time in the field for me," Will replied. "I thought I'd be psyched. But damn, got a weird feeling in the pit of my gut, you know?"

"It'll be all right," Brock said as he nodded. "We'll sync up after. You'll see."

Will looked across the roadway toward the dimly lit bar. "I'm in the breeze," he said, and took off, disappearing into the darkness.

Brock watched as Will moved out. Peyton walked up to him and watched as his facial expression hardened. Brock said, "Will and I have worked together on I don't know how many ops. He's saved my ass so many times I couldn't count them. But he's never once said he had a bad feeling about something." He shook it off. "Here," he said as he handed Peyton a tiny earpiece. "Put this in and listen closely to anything either Will or I tell you." She placed it into her ear and smiled. "You got the Glock? Let me see it." Peyton pulled the subcompact from behind her back. The silencer was already in place.

Brock inspected it, ensuring a round was in the chamber, then said, "Mags?" She held out five extra magazines, all filled with hollow point ammunition. "All right, give me about five minutes. I'm going to shimmy up the drainpipe on the back of this building and get up to the roof. Once I'm in position, and we confirm Will is in place, I'll give you the green light. Remember, get in and get out. Don't draw attention to yourself. Don't . . ." His words trailed off.

"What?"

Brock ran his eyes over her hair. "The hair."

"You like it? I dyed it black because I figured blonde would stand out too much."

He ran his fingers through it. "And this short cut. It looks good."

"Don't get any ideas, Mr. Paladin. They'll be time for that later."

He grabbed his gear and secured it on his back, then opened the door and stepped down. "There'd better be," he said with a smile.

Peyton watched as he grabbed the drain pipe and climbed straight up. He was over the top and onto the roof within seconds. She closed the door and walked to a bench seat in the back where she lifted the seat, revealing a hidden compartment. She knelt down and picked up a brick-shaped block, covered in tight, brown paper. The paper was stamped with:

BLOCK DEMOLITION
  COMPOSITION C4
   Lot #83776
   MFG DATE 7/28/2017

She took a knife and cut the block into four equal pieces, then picked up four detonator rods. She flicked the power switch of each to the "On" position to ensure the dim, red light emanated, indicating the devices had power and could be remotely triggered. She picked up the remote trigger timer and switched it on, then waited until the digital screen indicated that the device had radio-paired with each of the four detonators.

She thumbed the Up arrow and held it until the digital countdown readout said "30 seconds." She turned all the switches off, inserted one detonator into each C4 block, then picked up the remote trigger device and put it in her back pocket.

"Bring them out one at a time?" she said to herself. "I've got a better idea." She was on her own now, and it was time to end this thing.

50

RED AND FREE

Several minutes later, Brock was in position. He had chosen the southwest corner of the roof in which to lay. From there, he had the best vantage point from which to cover the rear of the bar building. And although he couldn't see the front, he had a partial view of the parking lot. He laid in a prone position, extended the tripod arms off the front of his sniper rifle's barrel and scanned the view. He made a few adjustments to the reticle and took inventory of the number of Harley's parked out front. "Eighteen, nineteen, shit, twenty." He keyed his headset. "Banger, this is six. I count twenty hostiles."

"Roger that, six," came Will's stilted reply. "Let's rock and roll."

"Roger that." And referring to the method used by factory workers start their shift, he said, "Time to punch the clock." He pressed his earpiece harder. "Shark bait, you ready for this?"

Peyton responded. "You two sound like a couple of old hens. Let's get this thing started."

Brock shook his head. "All hands, all hands, you are red and free."

Down in the RV, Peyton popped the door open without a second thought. She walked across the street underneath a broken street light, came over to one of the Harleys, then ran her fingers across the leather seat. She looked like a person who was window shopping.

* * *

As Brock watched, Peyton disappeared toward where the front doors were located. Brock keyed his headset. "Banger, the fox is in the henhouse."

"Roger that, six."

* * *

Inside the club, hardcore music thumped. The place was filled with the smoke of what looked like a thousand cigarettes. Peyton squinted through the dimly lit haze. When she smelled the distinctive scent of marijuana, she grinned and shook her head. "This is going to be too easy." There were dozens of bikers encircling the bar, each yelling for another round.

Peyton sat in a dark booth at the front of the club, removed one of the C4 charges from her vest pocket and pressed the putty underneath the table. The adhesive-like stickiness caused the waxy material to hold in place. She flicked the power switch, then got up and moved to the right side, found another empty booth, and repeated the process. About the time she flicked the power switch to the On position, a deep, guttural voice from behind her said, "Well would you lookey at what we have here."

Startled, she turned. The leather-clad biker's beer gut spilled out over his belt. His vest, adorned with patches, looked worn and tattered. He belched.

Peyton let her eyes run down his body. "You gonna sit down or just stand there trying to look down my bra?"

"My kind'a woman," the man said as he slid into the booth next to her. He ran a hand through his greasy hair as if his fingers were a comb. "Where you been all my life?" he said. His breath was nauseating.

"Just got into town," she said. "Passing through. Kind'a got thirsty." She looked between his legs. "Kind'a got a little more than thirsty."

He grinned, exposing yellowed teeth. "Like I said, my kind'a woman. You, ah, come in here just for a drink and a little . . . action?"

She took the half-full longneck out of his hand and tossed it back. "That takes care of one thing." She pushed him until he stood up. "Now, let's go take care of another."

* * *

Several minutes went by, and Brock shifted. He was fidgety, and he knew it. "Banger? You got eyes on?"

"Negative, six. I can't see shit in there. Just a closed rear door, no windows."

"Roger that."

"Just keep your pants on, compadre. She'll come through. You'll see."

"I'm going to raise her on the comm to make sure she's all right."

"That's a bad idea, compadre. Hey, wait a minute. You hear that?"

The sound of a chopper coming up the road became more audible. "Roger that, Banger. Got another Harley coming in."

"Just sit tight, six. Keep your focus. You have one job, cover the rear."

"Jesus, old man, you sound like—"

But just then the rear door of the bar popped open, and Peyton and a heavy-set biker spilled out. Brock clicked the reticle twice to zoom the night-vision scope closer, lined up the crosshairs, and flicked the safety off. He could see Peyton's face. She was grinning. She looked over her shoulder in Brock's direction and winked. Brock couldn't believe it. She turned her head to face the man again when Brock tapped off one round. The muffled rifle belted against his shoulder. The bullet zipped across the road and slammed into the man's forehead with a loud slapping sound. The man crumpled to the ground.

* * *

Grinder cut the engine to his Harley just as he saw a flash of light from the rooftop across the street, heard a muffled *whump*, then heard the loud slapping sound. He looked up. "What the hell was that?"

* * *

Behind the bar, Peyton's eyes flared wide as the man, who had been standing two feet from her, crumpled to the ground. Blood and brain matter had sprayed the dumpster behind, but in the darkness, no one could have noticed. She started laughing when Will called to her from the trees. "Hey! There ain't no time for that shit. Get your ass in gear. Focus on the job."

She looked in his direction but could see nothing through the inky blackness. "All right, Jesus. Girl can't have a little fun?"

She walked back inside, but this time, as the door swung open, light emanating from the club lit up the body, and Will knew he had to get it out of sight.

51

THE COUNTDOWN

Peyton let the steel door slam behind her. "That was fun, but not quite what I had in mind." Without hesitation, she walked around the right edge of the expansive room, past the pool tables, until she had reached the edge of the bar. She withdrew another small block of C4, concealed it in her hands, and pressed it firmly against the underside of the overhang, then switched the timer into the On position. "One more to go," she said to herself, then walked toward the pool tables.

* * *

Grinder slipped across the street and disappeared behind a building next to where Brock was positioned. He went around back and found the RV parked. "Wait a damned minute," he said as he cupped his hands around his eyes and looked through the rear windshield. When he could tell the vehicle was empty, he opened the door and stepped inside. He searched the RV, opening every compartment he could find, until, after throwing open a footlocker, he discovered something that confirmed his worst suspicions, several boxes of rifle ammunition. Each was marked:

Weatherby
  Cal .270 Weatherby Magnum

"Shit, shit, shit," he said as he went back out. He looked up toward the roof of the building but saw no way up. Then he ran to the next building over where he found an old fire escape ladder. He pulled against the rungs to check it, then went up as quickly and quietly as possible. He thought, *some mother fucker's up here. That was the flash of a muzzle I saw a minute ago. Dammit, that bitch is coming for us.*

The rear door of the club swung open and banged against the exterior wall. Will raised his rifle, and as if out of instinct, flipped the safety off. He could see Peyton with a big guy coming out. The problem was, the guy had his arm around her, and Will knew, neither he nor Brock would have a clear shot.

From the rooftop, Brock squinted into his scope. "Dammit, get out of the line of fire!" he said. But Peyton didn't. She braced the guy who kept wobbling from one side to the other. "Just let him fall!" Brock said. The biker began groping at Peyton, and the worst part was, she didn't stop him. Brock's heart rate accelerated. "Just shift him over. I swear if the son of a bitch hurts her." Brock's focus intensified. He had gone into tunnel vision. There was nothing else that could have gained his attention.

Grinder stepped onto the roof of the building next to Brock's and then quietly moved to the edge. His view was obstructed by a large air conditioning unit, so he moved further toward the front of the building. Finally, he saw what he'd feared, the barrel of a sniper rifle pointing in the direction of the bar. "Mother fucker," he said to himself. There was only about a ten-foot gap between rooftops, so Grinder took a dozen steps back, then ran full-speed and leaped across the opening. His feet touched home, and he rolled himself over to silence his landing.

Peyton pushed the big biker until he backed into the side of the building.

"You're not too drunk, are you?" she said as she ran her hand over his crotch.

"Oh, hell yes," he said. "Got me a wild one here."

She was so close to the guy, she knew Brock would never take the shot. And since Will was directly behind her, she knew he was cut off from firing as well. It was time for a little fun.

"You ever hear of zipper drills?" she said, her hand caressing between the man's legs.

"Zipper drills?" he said with a smile on his face. "Can't wait to find out what that is." He laughed.

Peyton used her left hand to unzip his fly, but with her right, she withdrew the Glock. She snap-fired four rounds into him, the first at zipper level, then consecutively higher until the last hit the top of his chest. It happened so quickly, the man barely had time to register before he collapsed. He began to moan and looked up at her, clutching his groin and gut in pain.

Peyton dropped the magazine out of the weapon and charged a fresh one. "Those are called zipper drills. You use them when you're close up to a subject and want maximum impact. They kind of get the point across, don't they?"

He groaned again and his eyelids crushed together.

"You fucking bitch," he said as blood frothed out of his mouth. "You shot me in the balls."

She knelt down and placed the barrel of the silencer into his throat. "You ever rape a woman?"

"Fuck you."

"Yeah, I bet you think it's funny as hell, don't you?"

He spat blood at her and groaned louder.

"Well, you'll never do that again." She stood and aimed at his face.

"Go to hell."

She tapped the trigger, and his head rocked back. He was dead. She slipped the gun inside her beltline, against her back, and heard Will's voice.

"What the hell are you doing?" he blurted.

"My job," she replied.

But then Will looked in Brock's direction and saw a silhouette on the roof behind him. "Oh, fuck!" Will raised his carbine and yelled out, "Brock!"

But it was too late. The man behind Brock had a gun in his hand and began shooting. There was no way Brock wasn't hit.

Will fired one round, which struck the man. But since Will's rifle was not fitted with a silencer, the report was deafening. The back door to the club was still wide open, and a commotion erupted inside. "Peyton!" Will called, as he jumped up. "Watch out!" then shoved her aside.

52

A ROOFTOP BRAWL

Brock recoiled, having been struck twice before Will had shot the man. The round from Will's rifle caught Grinder in the right shoulder. The gun dropped from his hand, and he went down. Brock rolled out of the line of fire as if out of instinct. He was injured, but the adrenaline exploded into his system, and he leapt up. His training kicked in. He didn't know where the threat had emanated, just that he was suddenly in a do-or-die fight.

He yanked a large dagger out of its sheath and jumped on top of Grinder. Grinder caught Brock's wrist, and the two struggled.

* * *

About a mile from the scene, Danny turned to Whelan. "Hey

Boss, we been at this for hours. I gotta take a leak. Pull it over, will you?"

Whelan shook his head and slowed the car, pulling it onto the shoulder of the road. "Rookies."

Danny opened the door and zipped his fly down. "Rookies? Come on L.T. I'm a detective. It took four years to hit this grade." Loud, popping sounds came from the distance. "You hear that, Boss?"

Whelan leaned out the window. "Shit! That's gunfire! Get in."

* * *

"What the fuck's goin' on out here?" yelled a biker from just inside the doorway. Just before several started to charge out, Will leveled the rifle at them and tapped off a few three-shot bursts, striking four in the process. Others inside the bar withdrew concealed pistols, and a firefight erupted. Will held his ground but was struck in the chest. He fell back.

"Will!" Peyton screamed as she ran to him. She picked up the rifle, shielded Will's body with her own, and opened fire. When the magazine emptied, she dropped it to the ground with mechanical smoothness, ripped open Will's daypack, and grabbed another. She charged the magazine into the receiver and popped the chamber closed, then moved to the doorway. She opened fire again, this time swinging the rifle right, then left, taking down two more bikers in the process. Several bikers dove for cover and began returning fire. Peyton looked back over her shoulder at Will. He wasn't moving. "Will? Will?" A round slammed into the cement block of the doorway just above her face. Bits of it peppered her cheek and jaw, and she recoiled. "Fuck," she muttered, then yanked out the one remaining block of C4 from her vest pocket. She armed the switch and threw it inside. "Screw you!"

Raising the rifle, she fired several more rounds which served to pin down the bikers inside. She pulled out the detonator device, clicked the button labeled ARM, then depressed the button labeled HOT. A digital readout displayed . . .

30 SECONDS

. . .and began to cycle down. Peyton fired several more rounds inside.

At the front of the club, John Michael Brewer ran for the exit as bullets zipped by. "Somebody's got a world of hurt coming to them!" he yelled as he leapt out the opening of the giant window he had broken earlier that day.

Peyton glanced at the timer.

24 SECONDS

She looked back at Will and rushed over to him. "Will, come on. We've got to get clear." She yanked his arm, but he would not move. "Will!" she pleaded. But Peyton knew, he was dead.

18 SECONDS

Peyton squinted in Brock's direction, then hip-fired her rifle several more times into the doorway. Across the street, she could see a blur of motion on the rooftop. Bullets from inside the club whizzed by her head, and she returned fire.

12 SECONDS

She grabbed at Will's arm and began to drag him. "Get up Will! We have to move." But no sooner had she pulled him a couple of feet when something slammed into the back of her head, and everything went black.

53

REVELATION

Gears towered over Peyton's unconscious body. "You mother fucking little cunt," he said. "I'm going to tear you limb from limb."

He grabbed her by the belt and yanked her up. The detonator dropped from her pocket, and he looked at it. On the face, he could read:

4 SECONDS, 3 SECONDS, 2 SECONDS . . .

He dropped her and started to run, but it was too late. All four C4 explosive charges detonated at precisely the same time. The explosive force blew cinder block walls down and destroyed the interior of the club. The front of the building collapsed, and glass shattered in all directions.

* * *

Inside the undercover police cruiser, Danny and Whelan's faces lit up as the ball of orange flame burst from the building. Whelan jammed on the brakes and the vehicle skid to a stop. "Christ. It's World War III out there!" Danny yelled.

* * *

As glass and shards of splintered wood rained down. Gears regained consciousness. The blast had knocked him out. He stumbled onto all fours and sat there a moment with his mouth hanging open. Blood oozed out both ears and from around his eye sockets. He looked back at the bar. The building was a total ruin, and he knew no one was still alive inside. He struggled to stand then wobbled his way back toward the spot where Peyton lay on the ground. He leaned down and picked up a large piece of broken plywood that was laying across her back. He took his boot and rolled her over, then stared at her face. "You," he said. "It's fucking you. That little cunt we've been looking for. I can't believe it." He pulled a stainless-steel Smith and Wesson .45 caliber automatic from his back and pointed it at her skull. He thumbed the safety catch and began to pull the trigger when a shot rang out.

Gear's body recoiled as the full impact of a hollow point .9 mm bullet struck him in the back, then passed through. He looked at his own chest, bewildered as blood began to pour free. With his gun still in hand, he turned around to find two men in business suits pointing guns at him. Whelan pulled the trigger twice more, and Gears went down. He was dead.

Danny kept his weapon up, not knowing if the threat had subsided, but Whelan knew, there was no one left alive inside. Danny ran toward the front, and Whelan called to him. "Call it in!" And referring to an ambulance, he added, "Tell them we need a bus. Tell them we need several buses."

Whelan pulled out his flashlight and examined Peyton's wounds. She was still laid out on the ground, but her eyes flickered, then opened.

"Shhh," he said. "It's over now. Just lay still. Help's on the way."

"Where's, where's—"

"It's all right now," Whelan replied. "You're Peyton Phoenix, aren't you? Where is Brock Paladin?" He looked through the smoke, his weapon still clutched in his hand.

"Brock, Brock," Peyton muttered. "I, I don't know."

"Was he inside when the explosion happened?"

"Why do you keep asking me about Brock?"

"He killed thirty people, and has apparently just blown up a building, that's why."

Peyton rolled onto her side, a reaction to the pain. "Why do you think Brock did this? He didn't do this; I did this."

Whelan's eyes widened. "What are you talking about? You couldn't have done this." His eyes traced the debris all over the ground. When he saw the detonator, he stood, then knelt down to retrieve it. He looked at it, then at Peyton.

Peyton saw what he was holding. "Detonator. I set the C4 inside, then activated it."

For a moment, Whelan was speechless. "This this yours?"

"Yes."

"You did this?"

"Of course, I did."

"But . . . how?"

"I've been trained. Did you think I was going to let those animals get away with it?"

The whole thing began to register in Whelan's mind. *They trained her.*

She began to regain her bearings. "But wait. Will, he's hit."

Whelan shined his flashlight across the debris until it landed on Will's dead body. "I'm sorry."

"Brock? Where's Brock?"

"Wait, is he here?"

She sat upright. "I feel like shit."

Whelan put his hand on her shoulder. "Tell me the truth. *Who* did all this?"

"I told you, I did. Brock and Will didn't want any part of it. But I was going to finish the job."

Whelan sat with the information a moment. "You came after them because of the attack?"

"Hell, yes, I did. Brock found me. And he found out the Lincoln Killers were coming after me. He took me and trained me. He wanted me to be able to defend myself. But I decided I'd take the fight to them instead."

"And it was you who killed all the men in that house? All thirty of them?"

"Yes, and I'd do it again. They thought they could rape me and throw me away like a pile of trash. Well, not anymore."

Whelan sat on the ground with his pistol now dangling in his hand. "I can't believe it. I was sure it was Brock Paladin."

She used his shoulder as a crutch and pushed herself to her feet. "I've got to find him. I've got to find Brock."

"Go," Whelan said.

"You're not going to arrest me?"

"Just go. In fact," he added, "you were never here."

Peyton ran into the darkness, across the street toward the building where Brock was.

54

DEPARTURE

Peyton stared at the rooftop but could see nothing. She ran around the side and called up, half whispering. "Brock? Brock?"

But she received no reply. She heard the sound of shuffling feet against the grit of roofing tar. Then heard a muffled yell. "Brock?" she called, much louder this time. The silhouette of two men at the roof's edge appeared, each gripping the other. It was so dark, the only thing Peyton could see were their outlines. One man reared his hand back, and Peyton saw a glimmer of steel, a knife. "Brock!" she screamed. But the man plunged the knife into the other. He pushed the wounded man until he flipped over the edge of the building, then slammed into the ground, head-first.

Peyton froze, looking at the darkened figure on the ground. She ran to him. "No, no, no . . ." She said as she rolled the body over in an attempt to see the face. In the

darkness, she could see nothing. The man gurgled something unintelligible. "Brock!" Peyton screamed as she shook
the man. She leaned her ear to his face and listened. The
breathing slowed, then stopped entirely. "Brock, no!"

Then a hand landed on her shoulder from behind. "You
trying to save him? I just got finished killing him." It was
Brock. She spun around and hugged him.

"Ouch, shit," he said.

"I thought, I thought that was you. I thought you
were dead."

"Nope, not quite, anyway." He leaned against her, and
she put her shoulder into his side for support. "Might need
a doc."

"God, you're bleeding," she said as she pulled him into
the dim light.

"I'll be all right. He snuck up on me, shot me twice, but
both just grazed me. Where's Will?"

Peyton said nothing, then looked down. "He's gone."

"Will's not gone. Maybe he got roughed up when that
building exploded, but he'll be all right."

"No, Brock, he's not. Will's gone. He died saving me. It
was my fault."

Police sirens could be heard in the distance.

"He can't be dead."

"Cops are already over there. He's gone, Brock, he's
gone." Peyton pushed him toward the RV. "There's nothing
we can do for him now."

Brock struggled against the emotions and physical pain

but allowed Peyton to help him into the vehicle. She lay Brock on one of the fold-down beds and then sat behind the wheel. She cranked the engine and pulled out, making a U-turn so they could drive behind the buildings and avoid being seen.

As the sound of sirens intensified, Peyton pulled the vehicle onto a side street and drove without headlights through the darkness. After several more turns, they were safely away. She pulled the vehicle off the road and went back to take a look at Brock's wounds.

He was becoming delirious. "Will, we have to go back for Will."

She shook his shoulder, and his eyes opened. "You've lost a lot of blood," Peyton said. She pulled his belt off of him and used it as a tourniquet to stave off the bleeding in his leg. "Here," she said as she moved his left hand onto the opposite shoulder. "Put pressure here. We've got to get you to a hospital."

"But they'll call the cops. GSWs are kind of a dead giveaway."

"It's either that or you'll die."

Peyton got back into the driver's seat and wove her way down the side roads, headed west and north through Pearland. As she pulled closer to the hospital, the building came into view, and she shivered. It was the same hospital she'd been brought the night she'd been attacked.

Instead of pulling up to the Emergency Room entrance though, she drove around the back of the hospital and parked against the building. "Brock? We're here."

Brock looked out the side window. "What are we doing around back?" he said as he sat up.

"I can't walk in the front door, not after what I've done."

Brock stood but then fell over. "Whoa, this is not good."

"No kidding. Like I said, you've lost a lot of blood. You've got to get help right now. But I can't go in there with you. I've got to go."

"No, babe, don't leave. Look, the cops aren't going to come after you. They'll pin it on me. I mean, it'll make perfect sense to them."

"No, they won't. I already told the detective I did it, that it was all my doing. When he comes to his senses, or when his superiors put two and two together, they'll know it was me."

"You can't go."

"It has to be this way," she said. "I'm sorry, Brock. I'm sorry about Will. Whatever you do, don't blame yourself. Will's death was all my fault." She stood and went to the side door, then looked back. "Don't try to walk. I'll call and have them come out and get you." She opened the door and stepped out.

"Peyton! Wait," Brock called. But she was gone.

55

TO VANISH IN PLAIN SIGHT

Pearland Medical Center

As Peyton crossed the dark parking lot and climbed a fence in the back, she pulled out her cellphone and looked up the phone number to the hospital, then dialed.

"Pearland Medical Center, how can I connect you?" the woman's voice said.

"Emergency Room, triage."

"One moment, please."

The call was answered. "Triage, this is Janice."

"This is an emergency. Is Doctor Ken Brantley in the hospital tonight? I need to speak to him immediately."

"Well, yes ma'am, he's here, but seeing patients and—"

"Get him," Peyton's tone was harsh. "It's a matter of life and death."

The woman hesitated, then said, "One moment."

About a minute later, Peyton heard, "This is Doctor Brantley."

Peyton's voice quieted. Just hearing his voice, the familiar voice of the physician that had kept her alive that awful night, then stopped by her room repeatedly while she was at the hospital, just to check up on her, took a toll. "Do you remember Jane Doe?"

"Jane Doe? We get a lot of Jane Does. Who is this?" But something in Brantley's voice turned. "Wait a minute, do you mean the Jane Doe that turned out to be named Peyton Phoenix? The woman that was saved by the Terminator?"

"Do you remember how I arrived at the hospital?"

"This is . . .?" he hesitated. "Of course, I do. You were placed inside a doorway at the back of the building so we would find you."

"I need you to go through that door right now," Peyton said as she skirted through some bushes behind an apartment complex a few blocks away. "Don't ask me any questions. Just do it. There's an RV parked there. Multiple GSWs. He needs your help right now or he'll die."

"I'll do it," he said, but the call had already gone dead.

Peyton took one last glance at the phone. As she continued her escape, she powered the phone down, dropped it onto the parking lot, then stomped it with her foot until it was smashed.

* * *

Six days later, Brock lay in his hospital bed. He glanced for the hundredth time at the handcuff attached from his wrist onto the steel bed rail. He heard voices outside his room, then a man in a crisp navy business suit and tie pushed the door open and walked in. The man's face was pockmarked, and Brock recognized him immediately. It was Lawrence Wallace.

"What do you want, Wallace?" Brock said.

"We've been looking for you a long time, Mr. Paladin," his voice, though laced with gravel, was more upbeat than usual.

"Yeah, well I left. I left the Agency."

"And now you're coming back." Wallace crossed his arms. "We've got work for you."

"You can forget it, Wallace. I'm never going back there."

"Oh no? Well, I suppose I could leave you here to rot. They're charging *The Terminator* with upwards of fifty homicides." He grinned. "Felony destruction of property, terroristic acts, weapons violations . . . Do you want me to go on?" He smiled again. "You know, you've got to love the media, don't you? The Terminator. It's so colorful, don't you think?"

Brock's jaw clenched.

Wallace's voice became distant, as one recalling a memory. "I much prefer *The Caiman*, don't you?" He walked to the window, his back to Brock. "The black caiman can grow up to sixteen feet in length and weigh upwards of twenty-four hundred pounds, yet they move like lighting. The true king of the Amazon basin. They have no natural predators." He turned to Brock. "Kind of like you."

"I'm not going back to that life."

Wallace leaned closer. "Of course, you are. You can either come back, or I'll next be visiting you in prison. The sentence would be, what, say, thirty years? Thirty years inside, a lifetime. Or we wheel you out of here right now."

Wallace was right, and that fact made Brock's stomach churn. Wallace turned to walk out. "There'll be some people here in a minute to take you out. See you back on The Farm, Mr. Paladin."

"What about the charges?"

Wallace stopped and looked back, then watted a dismissive hand across the leg of his trousers as if sweeping away a piece of lint. "Welcome back into the fold, Mr. Paladin. We've missed you."

"You're an asshole, Wallace," Brock yelled after him.

* * *

Twenty miles away, Peyton stared at her reflection in a dingy mirror in the restroom of the Alvin bus depot. She ran a handful of paper towels over her wet hair to dry it. She rinsed the sink out and disposed of the bottle of hair dye. This time, she had chosen sandy blonde—enough for a new look, but not enough to stand out. She donned a nondescript ball cap, pulled it low, then threw a small backpack over her shoulder. She walked into the station and melted into a group of people in line to board a bus. She flashed her paper ticket to the driver and found an empty row toward the back of the bus. A few minutes later, the bus pulled away from the station.

She was gone.

GET A FREE COPY

Get a Free Copy of
Protocol One

**Just visit NathanAGoodman.com/one/ for your free copy of
Nathan Goodman's runaway bestseller, *Protocol One*.**

The first casualty of terror is innocence

When Jana Baker first landed the internship of a lifetime,
she never imagined walking into a pit of terrorists. But when
a secretive federal agent approaches her, she learns the truth
and has no choice but to infiltrate their plot.

As the agent tries to protect her, Jana pushes past the outer
edges of peril only to find herself clinging for life.

Protocol One is the first book in Nathan Goodman's best-selling *Special Agent Jana Baker Spy-Thriller Series* and features high-adrenaline suspense, surprising plot twists, and a fiercely determined female heroine.

Pick up a copy free today and find out what 100,000 readers have already discovered.

Get your free copy at
NathanAGoodman.com/one/

www.ingramcontent.com/pod-product-compliance
Lightning Source LLC
Chambersburg PA
CBHW070446120726
47910CB00003B/950